THE OGRE OF OGLEFORT

Eva Ibbotson was born in Vienna, but when the Nazis came to power her family fled to England and she was sent to boarding school. She became a writer while bringing up her four children, and her bestselling novels have been published around the world. Her books have also won and been shortlisted for many prizes. *The Secret of Platform 13* was shortlisted for the Smarties Prize, and *Which Witch?* was runner-up for the Carnegie Medal. *The Ogre of Oglefort* was shortlisted for the Guardian Children's Fiction Prize and the Roald Dahl Funny Prize. Eva Ibbotson died peacefully in October 2010 at the age of eighty-five.

Books by Eva Ibbotson

The Beasts of Clawstone Castle
Dial A Ghost
The Great Ghost Rescue
The Haunting of Hiram
Monster Mission
Not Just a Witch
The Ogre of Oglefort
The Secret of Platform 13
Which Witch?

Let Sleeping Sea-Monsters Lie . . .
and Other Cautionary Tales

The Dragonfly Pool
Journey to the River Sea
The Star of Kazan

For older readers
A Company of Swans
Magic Flutes
The Morning Gift
The Secret Countess
A Song for Summer

THE OGRE OF OGLEFORT

EVA IBBOTSON

MACMILLAN CHILDREN'S BOOKS

First published 2010 by Macmillan Children's Books

This edition published 2015 by Macmillan Children's Books
an imprint of Pan Macmillan
20 New Wharf Road, London N1 9RR
Associated companies throughout the world
www.panmacmillan.com

ISBN 978-1-4472-6573-3

1 3 5 7 9 8 6 4 2

A CIP catalogue record for this book is available from
the British Library.

Printed and bound by CPI Group (UK) Ltd, Croydon CR0 4YY

For Laura

One
Gladys Says No

Most people are happier when their feet are dry. They do not care to hear squelchy noises in their shoes or feel water seeping between their toes – but the Hag of the Dribble was different. Having wet feet made her feel better: it reminded her of the Dribble where she was born and had lived for the first seventy-eight years of her life, and now she dipped her socks into the washbasin and made sure they were thoroughly soaked before she put them on her feet and went downstairs to make porridge for herself and her lodgers.

The Hag did not care for porridge – being fond of porridge is quite difficult – but she was glad to be busy; it helped her to cope with the terrible homesickness which attacked her each morning when she woke and saw the sooty brick wall of the house opposite instead of the wide sky and scudding clouds of the place where she had lived so long.

It is not easy to describe a Dribble. A Dribble is not exactly a marsh, nor is it really a bog or a water meadow, but it's a bit like all of these. Anyone who has been brought up in a Dribble suffers terribly when they have to leave; it is so quiet and so peaceful, and the damp air is so soft. You are never alone in a Dribble – there are frogs and newts under your feet, and birds wheeling overhead, and dragonflies

1

hovering over the pools, but often you do not see a human being for days on end.

Hags live for a very long time and she had expected to end her days there, and sink peacefully into the marshy ground when her life was done – but one day men had come with machines – more and more men and more and more machines, and had started to drain the Dribble and turn it into a building site.

So the Hag had come to London, not because she liked cities, she detested them, but because she needed to find work – and the work she found was running a boarding house for other Unusual People like herself – displaced witches or exhausted wizards or weary water sprites who had to do ordinary jobs because the time for magic seemed to be past.

The kettle had just come on to boil when she heard a noise like thunder coming from the room on the first floor where the troll was getting out of bed, and then a roar of fury. Ulf Oakroot also felt homesick when he woke up but his homesickness was not a damp, dreamy homesickness like the Hag's – it was a wild and angry longing for the forests of northern Sweden where he had been born.

Trolls are fierce and hairy, and extremely strong – and they have violent tempers. They can throw boulders for miles across fields and lift up small houses – but they love the woods in which they live and will do anything to protect them. So when the men had come with great saws and started to cut down the forests – not felling carefully – just destroying everything in their path, the trolls' world had been destroyed too. Ulf's brother had been killed trying to protect his home. And the men just came

2

with more lorries and bigger saws – until they had turned whole hillsides into a wasteland.

After the death of his brother, Ulf had left his homeland and taken a ship to Great Britain and moved into a room in the Hag's boarding house. Now he worked as a hospital porter, and because he was so strong and didn't put up with any nonsense, the patients loved him. No one was ever kept waiting on a trolley in the corridor when Ulf was on duty – he just put his huge hairy hand on the handle of the trolley and with a great cry of: 'Out of my way,' he shot off, with the patient shouting gleefully as they passed everybody else.

The Hag and the troll were good friends and by the time they had drunk three cups of tea they felt better. After all, when so many Unusual Creatures were going through bad times, losing their homes, doing jobs they would never have thought of doing in the olden days, it was wrong to grumble – and life at 26 Whipple Road was really not too bad.

'Where's Gertie?' rumbled the troll, spearing a sausage. 'Still in the bathroom, I suppose?'

The Hag nodded. 'She's had a bit of trouble with her lip. She tried to kiss a frog she found in a pet shop because she thought it might turn into a prince but it was the wrong kind of frog and she came up in awful blisters.'

The troll was not surprised. People were always being brought into the hospital with blisters from kissing the wrong kind of animal.

Gertie was an enchantress, though you wouldn't think it to look at her. She was a rather silly girl but she had a kind heart and the Hag was fond of her.

The other lodgers at Whipple Road were sisters, henkies – those faeries who limp and have hollow backs. They worked as dinner ladies in a school and were no trouble at all. There was also a man called Mr Prendergast, an absolutely ordinary man without a trace of magic in his blood. He had been living in the house when the Hag took it over and he saw no reason to leave.

They were all sitting round the kitchen table when the postman came by with an exciting letter. It was an invitation to the Summer Meeting of Unusual Creatures, which was just a week away.

Everyone was pleased. The Summer Meeting was important. It was there that they were told what the Holiday Task was going to be, and it was always something nice.

Last year they had all gone to the seaside at Southend to put the evil eye on a plague of jellyfish, which was bothering holidaymakers, and they had spent a happy week in the Grand Hotel. The year before they had gone to Scotland in two charabancs to deal with a gang of cattle rustlers which was threatening a herd of Highland cows. The scenery had been quite beautiful and everyone had come back feeling strong and well.

It was always fun, the Summer Task; it meant that they met all the other Unusual Creatures like themselves, and had a break from their daily lives. And the meeting gave them a chance to dress up a bit and show that they were still important.

'I'll go and tell Gladys,' said the Hag, 'so that she can prepare herself.'

Because the Hag was a kind of witch (most Hags

are, one way or another) she had a familiar – an animal that helped her with her magic. The Hag had brought Gladys with her from the Dribble and they had been together for years.

Gladys was a toad. She lived in the back yard under a stone and had grown fat on the worms and beetles that the Hag's lodgers brought her.

So now the Hag went out to give Gladys the good news.

'We're off to the meeting next week, Gladys,' said the Hag, and waited for her to come out for her worm and look pleased.

But Gladys did not move.

'Did you hear me, Gladys?' asked the Hag. 'It's the summer meeting on Saturday.' Gladys came out from under the stone. She came out very, very slowly. She opened one eye. Then she shut it again – and said a single word.

'Tired.'

'What do you mean, tired?' said the Hag crossly. 'I'm tired. Everyone's tired. London's full of people who are tired. They got tired in the war when their houses were bombed and food was rationed and all that, and they've been tired ever since. But we have to do our work.'

Gladys did not shake her head. Even toads who are familiars find it difficult to do that because their necks are so thick. All she did was repeat the same word.

'Tired.'

Gladys had never been a nice toad but this didn't matter. Familiars aren't meant to be nice, they are meant to be powerful. Now she turned her back on the Hag and began to crawl towards her stone.

'Are you telling me you aren't coming to the meeting?' cried the Hag.

Gladys did not answer but her back end looked obstinate and nasty.

'But I can't go without a familiar! It's impossible. I should feel undressed. I should feel stripped and naked!'

The troll shook his head. 'It's a bad business,' he said, 'but it's no good forcing her. She was always a bad-tempered animal. Goodness knows what she might get up to if you dragged her to the meeting against her will.'

'Yes, but what am I going to do?' cried the Hag.

'Could you perhaps get another familiar?' suggested Mr Prendergast. Being a completely ordinary person who worked in a bank made him see things very simply. 'There's a whole week to go.'

'A week's nothing,' cried the poor Hag. 'Oh, why is everything against me? Nothing's gone right since I left the Dribble!'

The other lodgers came out then and stood round looking worried. Once the Hag got upset she was apt to go downhill very fast and remember sad things like that she was an orphan. People are often orphans when they are eighty-two, but it is true that when you have no mother or father you can feel very lonely at any age.

But she was a brave person and soon pulled herself together – and the next day the hunt for a new familiar began.

Two

Finding A Familiar

The news that the Hag's familiar had gone on strike spread through the community of Unusual Creatures like wildfire. Gladys had never been popular and now everyone was bitter and angry that the toad had deserted her mistress just before an important meeting.

The Hag's friends did their best to help. The fishmonger, whose mother had been a selkie (one of those people that is a seal by day and a human at night) took her into the shop and offered her the pick of his fish. Not the dead fish on the slab, of course – a dead familiar would be very little use – but the live ones in a tank, which he kept for customers who liked their fish to be absolutely fresh.

'There's a nice flounder there,' he said.

But though flounders are interesting because they are related to the famous fish who reared out of the sea and granted wishes, the Hag was doubtful.

'It's really kind of you,' she said. 'But fish are so difficult to transport.'

Two witches, who worked as nannies, wheeling babies through the park, took her to Kensington Gardens because they had seen a tufted duck on the pond that they thought might be trained up to be magical. But when they found it they saw at once that it wouldn't do. It was sitting on a clutch of eggs and

7

looking broody and one thing that familiars never do is sit on nests and breed.

The next day the Hag took a bus to Trafalgar Square where she remembered having seen a pigeon with a mad gleam in its eyes. The Square was absolutely crammed with pigeons in those days but though she paced backwards and forwards among the birds for a whole hour, she couldn't find that particular bird again.

'We'd better try the zoo,' said the troll. So on his afternoon off from the hospital they took the bus to Regent's Park.

For someone looking for a familiar, the zoo is a kind of paradise. There were lynxes and pumas and jaguars, which seemed perfect – but the Hag knew that they would not be happy in the back yard of Number 26 Whipple Road, and though she was annoyed with Gladys, the Hag did not want her to be eaten.

There were cages of aye-ayes and lemurs and meerkats with huge eyes full of sorrow and strangeness, and there was a darkened room full of vampire bats and kiwis.

'A vampire bat would be wonderful,' said the Hag, and she imagined herself sweeping into the meeting with the blood-sucking creature dribbling on her shoulder.

But even in the zoo everything was not quite right. Not one of the creatures she saw really met her eye. The harpy eagles seemed to be half asleep; the serpents lay under their sun lamps and wouldn't move.

'Oh, what is the matter with the world?' cried the Hag when she got home again. 'It's as though nobody cares any more. When I was young, any animal worth its salt would have been proud to serve a hag or a wizard or a witch.'

They were sitting sadly at the kitchen table when there was a knock on the door and Mrs Brainsweller came to borrow some sugar.

'I've had so many funerals this week I hardly know which way up I am,' she said, 'and it's made me all behind with the shopping.'

Mrs Brainsweller was a banshee – one of those tall, thin feys who wail when people die and they are very much in demand at funerals. She could also levitate, that is to say she could float up to the ceiling looking down on the room, so she was a person who missed very little.

'You look a bit down in the mouth,' she said, when the Hag had fetched the sugar. So they told her what had happened at the zoo.

Mrs Brainsweller hit her forehead. 'Of course, I should have thought of it sooner,' she said. 'Bri-Bri will *make* you a familiar. There's nothing he couldn't do if he tried.'

The troll and the Hag looked at each other. Making familiars can be done but it is very difficult magic indeed.

Bri-Bri was the banshee's only son. He was a wizard – a small man with thin arms and legs and an absolutely enormous head almost entirely filled with brains. His name was Dr Brian Brainsweller and there was nothing he hadn't learnt. He had learnt spells for turning cows blue and spells for turning sausages into boxing gloves and spells for making scrambled eggs come out of people's ears and he had seven university degrees: one in necromancy, one in soothsaying, one in alchemy and four in wizardry.

But he didn't have any degrees in Everyday Life. Though he was thirty-four years old he was not good at tying his shoelaces or putting on his pyjamas the right way round, and he would have eaten furniture polish if you had put it before him on a plate.

Fortunately this didn't happen because Dr Brainsweller lived with his mother.

'What are you *doing*, Bri-Bri,' she would cry as he came down to breakfast with both his legs in one trouser leg, or tried to go to bed in the bath.

It was Mrs Brainsweller who had seen to it that Brian took all his wizardry exams, and stopped him when he wanted to do ordinary things like riding a bicycle or eating an ice cream because she knew that if you want to get to the top in anything you must work at it all the time.

The Brainswellers lived two doors down from the Hag's boarding house and Brian had a workshop in the garden where he spent the day boiling things and stirring things and shaking things. Though he was so shy, the wizard was a kind man, and he listened carefully, pushing his huge spectacles up and down, while the Hag and the troll explained what they wanted.

'Your mother thought you might make me a familiar,' said the Hag. 'It could be something quite simple – a spotted salamander perhaps?'

Dr Brainsweller looked worried.

'Oh dear,' he said. 'Of course if Mummy thinks . . . But I tried once and . . . well, come and look.'

He led them to a cupboard and pulled out a plate

with something on it. It looked like a very troubled banana, which had died in its sleep.

After that, the Hag lost heart completely. When she got back to her kitchen at Number 26, she found it full of friends who had come from all over the town to drink tea and tell her how sorry they were to hear of her trouble – and a retired river spirit, a man who now worked for the Waterboard, offered to climb into the drains and look for an animal that had been flushed down: perhaps a water snake or a small alligator which someone had got for Christmas and didn't want any more. But the Hag said it was now clear to her that she wasn't meant to have a familiar, and that The-Powers-That-Be intended her to be shamed at the meeting, if indeed she went to the meeting at all.

And when all her visitors had gone she put on her hat and smeared some white toothpaste on to her blue tooth and left the house. She wanted to put magic and strangeness behind her and talk to someone who belonged to a different world. Someone completely ordinary, and friendly – and young!

Three

The Boy

The Riverdene Home for Children in Need was not a cheerful place. It was in one of the most run down and shabby parts of the city. Everything about it was grey: the building, the scuffed piece of earth which passed for a garden, the walls that surrounded it. Even when the children were taken out, walking in line through the narrow streets, they saw nothing green or colourful. Although the war against Hitler had been over for years, the bomb craters were still there, and the people they met looked weary, and shuffled along in dingy clothes.

Ivo had been in the Home since he was a baby and he did not see how his life was ever going to change. He was not exactly unhappy but he was desperately bored. He knew that on Monday lunch would be claggy grey mince with dumplings, and on Tuesday it would be mashed potato with the smallest sausage in the world, and on Wednesday it would be cheese pie – which meant that on Wednesday the boy called Jake who slept next to him would be sick, because while cheese is all right and pies are all right, the two together are not at all easy to digest. He knew there would be lumps in the mashed potato and lumps in the custard and lumps even in the green jelly, which they had every Saturday, though it is quite difficult to get lumps into jelly.

He knew that Matron would wear her purple starched overall till Thursday and then change it for a brown one, that the girl who doled out the food would have a drop on the end of her nose from September to April, and that the little plant which grew by the potting shed would be trampled flat as soon as its shoots appeared above the ground.

Ivo's parents had been killed in a car accident; there seemed to be no one else to whom he belonged and he did his best to make a world for himself. There was an ancient encyclopedia in the playroom – a thick tattered book into which one could almost climb it was so big. And there was a well at the bottom of the sooty garden – covered up and long gone dry, but sitting on the edge of it one could imagine going down and down into some other place . . . and there was a large oak tree just outside the back gate which dropped its acorns into the sooty soil of the orphanage garden.

It was at the back gate that Ivo liked to stand, looking out between the iron bars on to the narrow street. Sometimes people would stop and talk to him; most of them were busy and only said a word or two, but there was one person – a most unlikely person – who talked to him properly and who had become a friend. The other boys always scuttled away when they saw her coming, and she certainly looked odd, but Ivo was always pleased when she came. She was someone who said things one did not expect and he did not know anybody else like that. The Hag did not have a grandson. She would have liked to have one but since she had never married or had any children it was not really possible. But if she had had one, she thought, he would have been like Ivo, with a snub nose, a friendly smile and intelligent hazel eyes. She had started by just saying hello to him on the way to the shops but gradually she had stopped at the gate longer and longer and they had begun to have some interesting conversations. Today, though, the Hag was so upset that she almost forgot she was talking to an ordinary human boy and one she had met only through holes in a gate, and almost straight away she said:

'I have had such bad news, Ivo! I have been betrayed by my toad!'

'By Gladys?' said Ivo, very much surprised. 'But that's terrible – you lived with her for years and years in the Dribble, didn't you? And you gave her your mother's name.'

'Yes, I did. You've no idea what I did for that animal. But now she won't do any more work. She says she's tired.'

There was a pause while Ivo looked at the Hag from under his eyebrows. He had guessed that Gladys wasn't just an ordinary pet but he wasn't sure what he was supposed to know and what he wasn't.

'I don't understand,' he said. 'I mean I thought . . . familiars . . .' He paused but the Hag didn't snub him or tell him to stop. 'I thought familiars didn't ever . . . I thought they served for life.' And under his breath, 'I would if I was a familiar.'

The Hag stared at him. She had never actually told him that Gladys was a familiar, but she wasn't surprised that he had guessed. She had realized all along that he was a most unusual boy.

'They do. They're supposed to. And it's such a bad

14

time . . .' It was no good holding back now. 'There's a meeting . . . of the London branch of all the people who are . . . well . . . not ordinary. And some of them think they are very powerful and special and show off like anything – even though the world is so different for people like us. If I go without a familiar they'll despise me, I'm sure of that,' she sighed. 'I suppose I must give up all idea of going. After all I'm so old and I'm an –'

She was about to say she was an orphan but then she remembered that Ivo was an orphan too . . .

But the boy was thinking his own thoughts.

'Can't you find another familiar?' he asked. 'There must be lots of animals who would be proud to serve you.'

'Oh, if only you knew, I've been everywhere.' And she told him of all her disappointments.

There was a long pause. Then, 'Why does it have to be an animal,' asked Ivo. 'Why can't a familiar be a person? They're just servants, aren't they – people that help a witch or a wizard?'

The Hag sighed. 'I don't know where I'd get hold of one. And they'd have to be trained . . . Though I suppose if it was just for the meeting . . . It might be rather grand to sweep in with an attendant. But it's too late now.'

Ivo was grasping the bars of the gate with both hands.

'I could be one,' he said eagerly. 'I could be your familiar. It says in the encyclopedia that they can be bogles or imps or sproggets and they're not so different from boys.'

The Hag stared at him. 'No no, that would never do.

15

You're a proper human being like Mr Prendergast. It's not your fault but that's how it is and you shouldn't get mixed up with people like us. It's very good of you but you must absolutely forget the idea.'

But Ivo was frowning . . . 'You seem to think that being a proper human is a good thing but . . . is it? If being a proper human means living here and knowing exactly what is going to happen every moment of the day then maybe it's not so marvellous. Maybe I want to live a life that's exciting and dangerous even if it's only for a little while. Maybe I want to know about a world where amazing things happen and one can cross oceans or climb mountains . . . or be surprised.'

'You mean . . . magic?' said the Hag nervously.

'Yes,' said Ivo. 'That's exactly what I mean.'

Four
A Meeting Of
Unusual Creatures

It was Ulf who persuaded the Hag to let Ivo come. As far as he could see it was only necessary to get her through the meeting: after the Summer Task had been given out she wouldn't worry so much about whether she had a familiar or not. So on the following day he tucked his long hair under a cap, the Hag wound a muffler round the fiercest of her whiskers and they went to see the Principal of the Riverdene Children's Home.

'We've just discovered that you have a boy here whose father we knew,' they told her.

And they asked if they could have Ivo to stay for a few days.

In those days it wasn't nearly so difficult to get a child to come for a visit and after they had filled in a few forms and produced a letter from Dr Brainsweller to say how respectable they were, Ivo appeared with a small suitcase.

'Only he must be back by Monday,' said the Principal.

Ivo was still wearing the dreary uniform of the Riverdene Home – grey shorts, grey sweater, grey socks – but his eyes were shining and as they took him back to Whipple Road it was all he could do to stop himself jumping for joy.

And it was clear from the start that he meant to

take his duties as a familiar very seriously.

'Oughtn't I to have . . . you know, tests? Inductions I think they're called?' he asked the Hag when she had shown him the attic where he was to sleep. 'Like . . . you know . . . having a live louse applied to my eyeballs. Or . . . swallowing a worm to show that I'm not squeamish. It could be a magic worm, the kind that tells you what to do from inside your stomach. I read about one in the encyclopedia.'

But the Hag said she did not keep lice in her house and the only worms went to Gladys, who had behaved badly but still needed to eat, and she set him to dry the dishes, which he did very well.

'Though I do wonder,' he said, 'I mean couldn't you just say a spell and the dishes would get dry by themselves?'

The Hag shook her head.

'You see, Ivo, there's a code about magic,' she explained. 'It mustn't be used for ordinary things like boiling an egg – things one can do quite well without it. People who use it for everyday jobs are looked down on, and rightly.'

'You mean it's a sort of force which mustn't be wasted?' asked Ivo, and the Hag nodded because that was exactly what she meant.

'And of course there are more and more of us whose powers are getting weaker,' she went on. 'I used to be able to give people smallpox when I was young and now I'd be hard put to manage even chicken pox. It's modern life. Switching on an electric light instead of waving a wand; aeroplanes instead of levitation; and all that scoffing and sneering. Our magic has been worn down by it.'

18

There were only two days now to the meeting but Ivo fitted in so well that it was quite difficult to remember that he was an ordinary boy and not an Unusual Person. Gertie had really taken to him; she had always wanted a little brother and she had made him a black cloak out of an old curtain, and they found a pointed cap for him in a dusty trunk. A proper grandson with Hag blood in him couldn't have looked better, they all agreed.

The Great Day had come and the party from Number 26 were in the kitchen, ready to leave for the meeting. The troll did not dress up but he had polished the staff of rowanwood which he had brought from his homeland. The Hag's other lodgers had gone to spend the night with friends and wouldn't be back till after the weekend, but Dr Brainsweller was there. His mother had brought him earlier and asked the Hag if she would take him to the meeting because she had to go north to wail at a funeral and she didn't think he would manage to get there on his own.

Then the door opened and the Hag entered. She wore a long Dribble-coloured dress: all the colours of water shimmered and blended in the velvet and she had polished her tooth.

And behind her came Ivo, in his black outfit, walking in her shadow as familiars should, but looking so attentive, so eager and intelligent, that everyone let out a sigh of relief. There was no possible danger of him being noticed and cast out as an ordinary boy, and they set off with glad hearts for the Hotel Metropole.

*

19

The Metropole was a luxury hotel in the centre of town, the kind with deep carpets and gilt-edged mirrors and interesting things for sale in the foyer. As they made their way upstairs, the Hag looked at Ivo a little anxiously because some of the people they mingled with really were rather strange: a fortune teller pulling along a large white gorilla on a lead; a family of fuaths (those tall faeries with green hair and a single eye) . . . a Strong Man from a circus dressed in glittering silver who had been dipped in a magic river when he was a baby so that no knife or bullet could pierce him . . .

But there was no need to worry about Ivo, the Hag soon realized. He was thoroughly enjoying himself. The big conference room on the first floor was filling up fast and the party from Number 26 slipped quietly into a row near the back. Everyone was whispering and talking among themselves, hoping that the Summer Task would be something far out in the country.

'I do so long for fresh air,' said an old brownie in the row in front of them.

There was a stage at the back of the room, and now the curtains swished apart and the organizer came on with a bundle of papers. Her name was Nellie Arbuthnot and she was a comfortable, homely sort of witch – plump, with a feathery hat. Her familiar was a parrot in a cage and she had slipped a green baize cover over it so that it wouldn't interrupt.

Nellie started by welcoming everybody and telling them that the refreshments in the interval would be served in the Blue Room across the corridor.

'The charge this year will be half a crown but you

will get value for your money, I promise you.'

Ivo turned his head as the Hag gave a small squeak of annoyance. 'I've forgotten my purse,' she whispered. 'I must have left it on the kitchen table.'

No one else from Whipple Road had any money. They would have to do without refreshments when the time came.

On the stage, Nellie shuffled her papers and cleared her throat. At the same time an assistant witch pulled down a screen and set up the magic lantern.

'You will want to know about the Summer Task,' Nellie said, 'and I'm happy to tell you that this year we have been asked to go to the Barber Holiday Camp in the New Forest and rid the camp – and in particular the fun fair which is attached to the camp – of a plague of mice.'

Murmurs of pleasure spread through the audience. A fun fair sounded good, and the New Forest was very beautiful. A picture of the camp now came on the screen. It looked really nice, with coloured chalets and well-kept flower beds. A picture of the fair came next with swings and roundabouts and a helter-skelter under a sunny sky – and then came one of the Barber family: Mr and Mrs Barber, and Penelope and Timothy Barber, nicely dressed children smiling into the camera.

'You may ask why the Barbers don't just bring in a lot of cats and the answer is that the family is allergic to cats. Cat fur brings them out in terrible bumps. So Mr Barber has invited us to spend a week as guests in his camp, and concentrate in particular on the fun fair where the mice are breeding at a terrifying rate. He leaves it to us how we get rid of the mice –

shape-changing . . . luring . . . the evil eye . . . Leading them into a hill like in the Pied Piper of Hamlyn is of course a possibility.'

She waited for a moment while the tired creatures who had worked all summer in the city, talked delightedly among themselves. This was going to be the best Summer Task ever!

'Now we come to the arrangements for the journey,' began Mrs Arbuthnot. 'We will travel from –'

But at that moment something extraordinary happened. The curtains swished together. The lights flickered and went out. An icy draught crept through the room – there was a single roar of thunder, followed by complete silence.

And then . . . from behind the curtains . . . came a slow and eerie noise.

Creak . . . creak . . . creak.

The lights came on again. The curtains parted, but there was no sign of Nellie Arbuthnot or her parrot. Instead, on the stage, was a most extraordinary contraption. A gigantic circular bed on wheels. A movable hospital bed? A death bed? Nobody knew . . .

And on the bed crouched three women.

But what women! They were older than time with cracked and hideous faces, tangles of long white hair and a ghastly stare.

Panic spread through the audience. The Hag took Ivo's hand; she was clammy with fear.

'Norns!' The terrified whisper could be heard all over the room. 'It's the Norns! It's the Old Ones!'

Norns are the eldest Beings in the world. They were there at the beginning of time and they never

22

quite die. Anyone who sees them feels an unstoppable dread because the Norns are the Fates; they spin the threads of the future and foretell what is to come.

The frightful things crouched on the bed, peering at the rows of people watching them. At the same time, on the screen behind them, the cheerful faces of the Barber family vanished – and instead there appeared a landscape of towering black cliffs, lashed by a stormy sea. White spray dashed against the rocks; they could hear the howling of the wind.

The picture moved inland through a cleft in the cliffs and stopped in front of an enormous castle with turrets and towers and places for pouring boiling oil. The windows were barred with iron; black birds circled the battlements.

Again the picture changed. They were inside the castle now, in a huge banqueting hall, its walls hung with death-dealing instruments and the antlers of slaughtered animals. And then came gasps and cries of 'Oooh' from the audience – because what they were seeing was a head.

But what a head! Swollen and loathsome, with hate-filled eyes, a pock-marked nose . . . a mouth opened to show blood-stained teeth.

The Norns pointed to the picture with their deformed fingers.

'It is the Great Ogre,' intoned the First Norn.

'The flesh-eating Ogre of the North,' pronounced the Second Norn.

'The dreaded Ogre of Oglefort,' uttered the Third Norn.

For a moment the camera stayed on the fearful head. Then it pulled back to show the figure who knelt at the monster's feet: a young girl with long hair streaming down her back, her hands clasped beseechingly. But just as the ogre's hands came down towards the trembling girl, the screen went dark.

'It is the Princess Mirella,' said the First Norn in her sing-song voice.

'She must be rescued,' said the Second Norn.

'Saved,' said the Third.

'And the ogre must be slain,' said Norn Number One.

'Killed,' said the Second Norn.

'Pulverized. Absolutely,' said the Third.

Then all three of them pointed to the audience and with one voice they cried:

'THIS IS THE TASK!'

A rustle of despair went through the Unusual Creatures.

'What about Mr Barber's Holiday Camp?' came a voice from the back.

The great bed shook as the fearful females rose to their knees.

'THE TASK IS GIVEN,' screeched all three Norns again. 'And any waverers will feel the pull of Hades.'

They fell back on their pillows. Rattling noises came from their throats. The nurses who had brought them in wheeled the bed to one side of the stage, and Nellie Arbuthnot came back, looking shaken. The parrot in its cage had fainted.

'If you make your way to the refreshment room, we will prepare the instructions for the . . . er . . . the ogre-slaying,' she said nervously. 'You have half an hour.'

The curtains were pulled together and everyone

24

in the audience trooped out of the room – everyone except the people from Number 26 who had no money.

'This is terrible,' whispered the Hag to the troll. 'I'd never have brought the boy if I'd known what was going to happen.'

But Ivo did not look frightened. He looked excited.

Behind the curtains, the nurses came with large syringes to inject the Norns, and pills to push down their throats.

The minutes passed.

Then a bell rang, the signal that the meeting was going to start again. There was the noise of footsteps of all kinds coming from the refreshment room, but none of them seemed to be coming back into the hall. One could hear the sound of slithering and limping and shuffling which gradually grew fainter – and then silence. Every one of the Unusual Creatures had made their way down the stairs and out into the street, heading for home.

The curtains parted. The Norns were a little stronger after their injections; they knelt up in the great bed and raked the room with their baleful eyes.

What they saw was a Hag and her familiar, a troll, a small wizard – and nobody else.

The Norns beckoned to a nurse and stuck out their arms and she gave each of them another injection from her huge syringe – but it made no difference. When the Old Ones peered into the room once more they still saw only the same four people.

There was nothing to be done, and the Norns made the best of it.

'You are the Chosen Ones,' said the First Norn.

'You are the monster-slayers,' quavered the Second.

'The rescuers,' said the Third.

'But –' began the Hag.

She had infuriated the ancient creatures.

'There is no BUT,' screeched the First Norn.

'No BUT whatsoever,' yelled the Second.

'Not anywhere is there a BUT,' cackled the Third.

The bed shook with their rage.

'The others have failed the test,' they pronounced. 'On you falls the Glory of the Task. You are the ogre-slayers.'

The room went dark. There was the eerie creak again as the great bed was wheeled away. And the party from Number 26 were left alone.

Five

The Briefing

'I think we need a nice cup of tea,' said the Hag when they returned from the meeting.

But even after three cups of tea and five slices of bread and butter in the kitchen of Number 26, they still felt terrible. One minute they had been looking forward to Mr Barber's Holiday Camp – and the next they were branded as ogre-slayers and given this appalling task.

'It's because there's a princess involved,' said Ulf gloomily. 'That's why the Norns appeared. Princesses always bring them out.'

The wizard was worrying about his mother.

'She won't like it. She won't like it at all,' he muttered.

'I don't know how to slay things,' said the Hag in a worried voice. 'It's not what I do.'

Ivo put a hand on her arm. 'But think what an exciting adventure it'll be. And we won't only be slayers – we'll be rescuers. Rescuing the princess has to be good.'

'Not for you, it doesn't,' said the Hag sharply. She was still feeling very guilty because she had let Ivo become mixed up in something so dangerous. 'You won't be a slayer and you won't be a rescuer; you're going back to the Home first thing on Monday.'

'No I'm not,' began Ivo. 'I'm a familiar and –'

But at that moment there was a loud pecking noise at the window, and looking up they saw, caught in the rays of the street lamp, a large black bird, perched on the sill. The Hag was just going to open the window when the bird flew *through* the glass panes, circled the room, dropping evil-smelling black feathers, and settled, with its unpleasant-looking feet, on the butter.

'A harpy,' said Ulf, looking at the creature's swivelling yellow eyes. Harpies are messengers from the Underworld and have to be taken seriously. 'What can we do for you?'

The bird did not answer. Instead it opened its beak, let a piece of paper fall on to the table and flew off again, through the unopened window.

While the Hag scooped the butter into the dustbin, Ulf read out the message.

In strange wavery letters it said:

ALDINGTON CRESCENT UNDERGROUND STATION – MIDNIGHT TONIGHT

Everyone looked at everyone else.

'That station's been shut forever since the end of the war,' said Ulf. 'It was badly bombed, and the whole line's been disused. We can't go there.'

'But we have to,' said the Hag. 'It'll be the briefing – telling us what to do. You'll have to wait here for us, Ivo. I'll leave a night-light on and –'

'No!' Ivo's voice was very strong. 'You said you wanted a familiar and you've got a familiar. Familiars serve for life, I told you. I'm coming.'

'But –'

'Let the boy come,' said Ulf. 'He's too far into it now. On Monday he can go back.'

It was as the troll had said. The station entrance was sealed off by a great iron gate covered in rust. It looked as though it had been there forever.

'Well that's that,' said the Hag. 'We'd best be getting back while the buses are still running.'

But Ivo had gone up to the gate. He put a hand on the lock – just touching it – and now slowly, creakily, the gate began to open, only a crack at first . . . then all the way.

'I don't like this,' said the wizard. 'I don't like it at all.'

Nobody liked it, but keeping close together they made their way down a flight of steps into a freezing and derelict ticket hall. The machines were wreathed in cobwebs; a torn poster said 'Dig for Victory' – which was what people had been told to do in the war.

'This used to be the deepest underground station in London,' said Ulf.

They huddled together wondering what to do next. Then a faint blue light came on above a sign which said: 'To the Trains.'

But of course there weren't any trains. There hadn't been any trains for years. The notice led to what seemed to be a hole in the wall but was actually the top of a curving concrete staircase.

'They want us to go down there,' said Ivo.

But who were they? There was no one to be seen.

They began to walk down the stone stairs and all the time it got colder and colder.

'I didn't know there were so many stairs in the world,' said the Hag.

They reached the bottom at last and found themselves on a platform with a row of broken-down sweet machines, and some battered wooden benches. There was a smell of decay and oldness.

'Now what?' wondered the troll. 'We can't go any lower.'

And then, incredibly in this station which had been closed for years and years, they heard the sound of a train!

The sound came closer. The train appeared in the mouth of the tunnel. It slowed down but it did not stop. In the dim light inside the carriages sat rows of dark-clad spectres, staring at the ground.

'A ghost train!' said the wizard. 'Who would have thought it?'

Ivo felt a chill run through him; he'd never seen ghosts before.

The train moved off. The monster-slayers waited in eerie silence.

After a few minutes the ghost train reappeared; the same dark spectres sat staring at the ground. They were on a circle line, doomed to go round and round forever.

Once again the ghost train vanished into the tunnel; once again the slayers waited. Then for the third time they heard the noise of a train, but this one did not only slow down, it stopped and a disembodied voice said, 'Enter.'

It took a lot of courage to get into the train. The seats were ripped and covered in harpy feathers; rats scuttled about on the floor.

The doors shut. The train began to move.

They went through a number of stations. On one, the sign said 'River Styx'. Another said 'Medusa's Lair'. It looked as though the Underworld had taken over the underground.

Then the train slowed down, stopped. The doors slid back and the poor slayers, frightened and bewildered, got out.

They were in a kind of hollow cave. The smell was vile; harpies roosted on the ledges, water dripped from the roof.

But on a platform in the centre of the cave was something familiar: the Great Bed of the Norns – and all three of the Old Ones were there, leaning against the pillows.

For a moment the Norns stared with their bleary eyes at the group of people coming towards them. Then they shook their heads. They had forgotten how bad it was.

There was a pause, and because it looked as though the Norns might drop off to sleep the troll said, 'You have orders for us?'

The Norns sat up. 'Orders,' they agreed. 'And gifts.'

They clapped their hands and one of their attendants came forward carrying a leather pouch full of black beans. Beans are often magical and these were very magical indeed because they enabled the person who had eaten one to understand the speech of anyone they were talking to, whether it was a human or an animal.

The slayers thanked them and the Hag put the pouch carefully in her handbag.

31

The second gift was a ketchup bottle filled with a yellowish liquid.

'Foot water,' said the First Norn.

'Water in which feet have been washed,' said the Second Norn.

'Feet of heroes,' said the Third Norn.

The wizard took it and asked shyly what the foot water was for.

'Wounds,' said the First Norn.

'Heals wounds,' agreed the Second.

'Usually,' said the Third.

But gifts from people who deal in magic nearly always come in threes, and now the Norns clapped their hands and one of the attendants came forward carrying a rusty sword.

The Norns had ordered it when they'd realized that not one of the slayers had a proper weapon.

'For plunging,' said the First Norn.

'Or thrusting,' said the Second.

'Or stabbing,' said the Third.

'Into neck of ogre,' said the First Norn.

'Or stomach,' said the Second.

'Or chest.'

The attendant continued to hold out the sword, but no one moved. The troll was strong and brave but he worked with wood, not rusty metal – and the wizard thought that the sword looked heavy and carrying it would make it difficult for him to think. Then Ivo stepped forward, and held out his arms, and the attendant laid the sword across them.

The Norns were very tired now. Their heads kept falling forward on their skinny necks and they shook themselves awake. Then they beckoned once again, and another of their attendants came with a small packet.

'Open later,' whispered the First Norn.

'At home,' croaked the Second.

And a few moments later, the cave resounded with their snores.

The packet, when it was opened in the kitchen of Whipple Road, did not contain a phoenix or a dragon's egg. It was a pleasantly ordinary parcel. Inside was a large map of the island of Ostland surrounded by ocean. A rocky bay on the northern tip of the island was marked with a black arrow.

There was also a page of instructions for the journey – and four envelopes. Each envelope had on it the name of the person who was to travel. One said Hilda Garbuttle, which was the official name of the Hag. One said Ulf Oakroot; and one was made out to Brian Brainsweller. Inside each of the envelopes was a train ticket to Rylance on Sea and a boat ticket from there to Osterhaven, the most northern port on the island.

'There's an extra envelope,' said the Hag.

The troll picked it up. Quite clearly it was labelled: 'Ivo Bell.'

'Oh but he mustn't come,' began the Hag. 'He absolutely mustn't be allowed to run into danger. I'll rub out his name – we can get the money back perhaps?'

She found a rubber – but as soon as she started to remove Ivo's name, the letters came back again, as clear as day.

'Better not meddle with the arrangements, Hilda,'

said the troll. 'Who knows, they must have seen something in the boy.'

Ivo had the sense then to go quickly up to the attic and put himself to bed. But he was far too happy to go to sleep. Tomorrow, the day when he would have sat down to claggy mince and lumpy custard, he would be setting off on an amazing adventure.

Ostland . . . He had heard of it of course; an island as big as England and Scotland and Wales all put together, afloat on a remote and mysterious ocean. Ivo had longed to see it, poring over maps in the encyclopedia, but he had never dreamed that he would make the journey. And he was going to rescue a young girl from dreadful danger! He could see her now, kneeling in terror before the great beast which threatened her. It was a pity she was a princess – Ivo did not approve of people being royal – but it was not her fault; one cannot choose one's parents.

And all this because a toad called Gladys had said 'no'.

Six

Mirella

Ostland is an unexpected place. The south of the island is peaceful. It has a string of pretty towns along the coast and the biggest of these, which is called Waterfield, is the capital. In Waterfield you can find everything you can find in London or Dublin – or even in New York. There are the Houses of Parliament and the law courts and theatres and a zoo – and because the town lies by the sea there is a harbour for big boats and a marina for smaller ones.

If one goes further north towards the centre of the island one comes to rich farming land. Here there are orchards and studs for breeding racehorses and beech woods carpeted with bluebells.

But the very north of the country is different. Completely different. There was an earthquake in Ostland many hundreds of thousands of years ago and it made a deep cleft across the northern tip of the island which cut it off from the rest of the island. On the far side of the cleft the land is rocky and wild and almost empty. At least it is empty of ordinary people and ordinary houses. But in the folds of the dark hills are caves and castles and tunnels and the people who live there would not be found in any telephone book. This part of the island is only connected to the rest of the island by a narrow bridge across a ravine which is hundreds of feet deep. But even if the bridge were wider and the ravine less deep, the people from the friendly civilized part of Ostland would not have tried to cross it. One of the first things the children of Ostland heard from their nursemaids and their parents was what would happen to a child foolish enough to try to cross the bridge to the north. Sometimes their legs would be torn off and thrown into the ravine, or their eyes would be pecked out . . . and if they got across there would be all sorts of delightful people waiting for them, ready to turn them into bluebottles or nail them to trees or pull them down into fiery pits.

Although the citizens of Ostland spoke English, they refused to have a monarchy. They didn't want to have a king and queen ruling over them and bossing them about.

All the same there was a palace in Waterfield – a big one, lived in by a royal family called the Montefinos. They had come to the island many years ago and nobody minded because a palace is a colourful thing to have and it was good for tourists to have something to photograph. There were also a few castles scattered around the south where dukes and princelings spent their time hunting or gardening or playing whist.

Though the Montefinos did not actually rule over the country they were very grand. They kept their own sentries and bodyguards and had over a hundred servants. They drove about in carriages with their crests on the door and they waved graciously to the people with their white-gloved hands. They opened bazaars and had their portraits painted and gave balls, and rode thoroughbred horses in the park with their grooms cantering behind them.

The Montefinos had three daughters. Princess

Sidony was the eldest; then came Princess Angeline, and a long way behind them came the youngest, Princess Mirella.

Sidony and Angeline were pretty, obedient girls who liked doing all the things that royal people do, but Mirella did not. She was a misfit from the start. Mirella did not look like a princess. Her eyes were black and her hair was straight and her ears stuck out. Mirella would not ride in a closed carriage and wave to the people; she said driving made her sick. She would not have her portrait painted or go and play with children who were 'suitable'.

What Mirella was passionate about was animals. Not just cats and dogs and horses but creatures most people hardly know are there. She had made a sanctuary for woodlice and ground beetles and earwigs in a courtyard garden. She kept a plaster of Paris ants' nest under her bed and when the maids tried to remove it she threw a tantrum which echoed through the palace. Her dog was not a beautiful saluki like the dog that was photographed with Princess Sidony, or a perfectly groomed Afghan like the dog owned by Angeline – it was a stray she had made her bodyguards pick up on the way to the dentist: a rough-coated mongrel with a funny eye. She called it Squinter and her mother shuddered whenever she caught sight of it.

And she had a passion for birds. While she was still in her pram she had looked for hours at the starlings and sparrows and chaffinches that came close. By the time she was seven there was hardly a bird she did not recognize and when her nursemaid took her down to the harbour, the little girl couldn't take her eyes off the gulls and terns and gannets wheeling over the water.

'They're so *white*,' she said to the nurse.

One of the things that royal families like very much is having weddings, and on the day she was eighteen Sidony got engaged to Prince Philippe who lived in a slightly smaller palace along the coast.

He was a very uninteresting young man who lived for his stamp collection, but both families were pleased and a great wedding was planned to take place in Waterfield Cathedral.

'You're going to be one of the bridesmaids, dear,' her mother told Mirella.

'Do I have to be?' asked Mirella, which upset her mother because surely all normal little girls want nothing more than to go down the aisle in a pretty dress.

The wedding was incredibly grand. The church was decorated with a thousand pink roses and Sidony wore a cream gown with a nine-foot train. Mirella's dress was embroidered all over with tiny pink rosebuds.

'You're going to look so sweet, my darling,' said her mother.

'No, I'm not,' said Mirella. 'I'm going to look like an escaped measles rash.'

But everything went off pretty well except the usual things – an usher being sick on the best man's shoe, a mouse in the trifle . . .

After that Mirella had two years of peace during which she set up a freshwater aquarium with nesting sticklebacks and tamed a jackdaw that had fallen down the chimney. And then Angeline got engaged to the only other prince in Ostland – a weedy young man who sucked peppermints all day long because he worried about his breath. So Mirella had to be a bridesmaid once again.

This time the wedding was even grander. The bride carried a huge bouquet of hyacinths, which matched her eyes, and the bridesmaids wore silver dresses covered in glittering sequins.

'Like fish,' said Mirella.

But she was fond of fish and behaved well.

Once again there were a couple of years of peace – and then Mirella's parents started to worry. The supply of princes in Ostland had now run out so where were they to find a husband for their youngest daughter?

'Of course she's only a child,' said her mother. 'She can't marry for years but we've got to make sure there's someone ready for her when the time comes.'

So Mirella's parents went prince hunting in Europe and after many disappointments they found the Crown Prince of Asmora, a small country between Italy and France, and the prince was invited to Waterfield to come and look Mirella over.

The visit was not a success. Prince Umberto arrived a day before he was expected and instead of finding Mirella in her best dress with her hair curled, he found her in overalls cleaning out her stickleback tank. Her hair was screwed up in two rubber bands and there was waterweed all down her front.

Prince Umberto did not at all take to Mirella and she most certainly did not take to him. He was a conceited show-off with a silly blond beard and a sneery voice.

'You'll have time to get used to him,' said Mirella's mother.

But Mirella said she wouldn't get used to him in ten years or in twenty or a hundred. 'You can hang and draw and quarter me before I'll join my life to that oik,' she said.

So the prince went away but that was not the end of the matter. Mirella's father was very rich – he owned oil wells and diamond mines – and Prince Umberto's father was poor and he told Umberto that he had to promise to marry Mirella as soon as she was old enough.

'I'll do it,' said Umberto, 'but she's got to be cleaned up and turned into a proper princess. I'm not living with fish and mongrel dogs and jackdaws.'

Mirella's parents saw his point, and they began to train Mirella. They confiscated the ants' nest. They took away the aquarium. They shooed out the jackdaw. And they said that the little dog would have to go before the prince's next visit.

'We'll get you a beautiful pedigree dog like your sisters have,' they told her.

'I don't want a pedigree dog, I just want Squinter,' said Mirella. 'Please let me keep him. Please.'

But it was no use. Mirella fought and argued and threw tantrums but one day she came back from a walk and found that the little dog was gone.

'We're doing this for you,' said her parents. 'So you can become a proper princess.'

It was then that Mirella realized just how helpless children really are.

40

When she was very unhappy, Mirella used to climb out of a window on the top floor of the palace and crawl along the battlements to a place where she could watch the clouds and the wheeling birds, and after a while she usually felt better.

The day after the little dog had gone, Mirella clambered on to the roof and lay there.

She had always found it easy to follow the birds with her eyes and feel as though she was one of them, but today, because she was so wretched, the feeling was so strong it overwhelmed her.

A seagull mewed and whirred over the chimneys, and the sun caught its dazzling plumage. A pair of terns in from the sea swooped so low that she could see the pupils of their eyes – and high among the clouds a kestrel was hovering.

And as she lay there Mirella felt as though she too was winged and completely free . . . A white bird in a pale blue firmament, not thinking or worrying or afraid – just feeling the wind currents beneath her wings and flying on and away . . . on and on . . .

It was in so many of the stories . . . the magic birds who flew high above the earth, seeing the silly worries of people below dwindle away. The wild geese who carried the boy Nils on their backs across the whole of Sweden . . . The Great Roc who bore Sinbad away to the Valley of Diamonds . . . The swallow who took Thumbelina to Africa.

Except that if she was a bird she wouldn't carry anyone in her claws. She would fly away higher and higher, as far as she could go – but alone. Always alone and free.

After an hour her old nurse became worried and the palace was searched and a pageboy fetched her off the roof.

As soon as she saw the princess, the nurse began to scold.

'You know you're not supposed to go up there. You'll fall to your death gawping at those dratted birds. The way you carry on you'll become a bird yourself one of these days.'

Mirella never really listened when her nurse started to scold, but now she said, 'How could I? No one can become a bird.'

'Oh can't they just,' said the old woman. 'There's sorcerers and monsters enough in the north to turn people into worse than birds.'

'What sorcerers?' asked Mirella. 'What monsters?'

But the nurse wouldn't say any more – she had been forbidden to frighten Mirella with stories of what went on in the far north of the island.

'What sorcerers? What monsters?' repeated Mirella. 'You're making it all up.'

'I am not,' said the nurse angrily.

That was all she would say – but it was enough. All the next day and the day after, Mirella was very quiet and absent-minded.

And on the third day the servants found her bed empty – and not a trace of her in the length and breadth of the palace.

Seven

The Journey

The small, black-painted boat sailed over the dark water. The old man in oilskins who steered it was grumpy and silent. Occasionally he looked at Ivo and shook his head.

They had reached the last stage of the journey. They had followed the Norns' instructions and everything had gone as it should: the ferry had taken them to the most northern port in Ostland, and after a night in a boarding house by the quayside they made their way to Pier Number Three where an old man in his clinker-built fishing coble seemed to be expecting them.

When they were clear of the harbour the old man began to mutter.

'You'd best say your prayers,' he said. 'There's some dangerous ogres along this strip of coast but the one where you're going's the worst. There's no one comes out of that place the way they went in.'

Ivo knew he should be afraid. What they were trying to do wasn't just dangerous it was probably impossible – but the only thing he'd been afraid of all along was that the Hag would find a way of sending him back.

The north shore of Ostland is famous for its rough seas. As they came out of the shelter of the harbour the boat started pitching and tossing and first the Hag and then the troll turned green and leaned over the side, ready to be sick. From time to time they were drenched by bursts of spray but felt too wretched to care. Ivo and Dr Brainsweller did not feel ill – they sat back in the stern, hypnotized by the rise and fall of the waves.

They had travelled for more than two hours when there was a sudden gasp from the wizard.

'L-look,' he stammered, clutching Ivo's arm. 'Up there! It's Mother!'

And it was. High above the heaving boat there floated a long, pale face. A pair of rimless spectacles clung to its pointed nose – its lips moved and formed a single word.

'Bri-Bri?' said Mrs Brainsweller above the noise of the wind, and vanished.

The wizard was terribly shaken.

'You did see her?' he asked. 'I didn't imagine it?'

And Ivo had to admit that he had indeed seen Mrs Brainsweller's worried face.

'I don't suppose she'll come again,' he said. 'She just wanted to see if you were all right.'

After another hour the boat came in closer to the shore, the water became calmer and wearily the others raised their heads. They were sailing along a spectacular coastline of high jagged mountains and sheer cliffs. There were no harbours, no villages, only the sea birds swooping and crying: guillemots and kittiwakes and terns . . .

'How can we land?' wondered the troll.

The grumpy boatman did not answer. And then they saw a gap in the cliffs, and a small sandy bay with a rickety-looking jetty.

'Is this it?' asked the Hag. 'Are we here? But there's no castle.'

'It's inland – you have to walk up through the trees.' And then: 'I'll take you back if you like. It's a pity to see the little lad going to his death.'

But it was too late for that. They climbed stiffly out on to the jetty and down on to the sand. In front of them lay an opening fringed by bushes. It had begun to rain.

They were wet through and tired even before they began their trek inland through the trees and along the overgrown path. It ran beside a small and sluggish stream covered in water weeds and green slime. Every now and again a blister of gas came to the surface with a sinister plop.

'Methane,' said the troll.

The trees grew gradually taller as they walked away from the sea. They leaned towards each other; lichen hung down from the branches. The birds that screeched above them now were not white like the sea birds, but black – rooks and jackdaws and crows.

In the mist and rain it could have been any time of day.

'Oh dear,' said the wizard. He had stepped on a heap of toadstools oozing something yellow, like pus.

Ivo carried the sword over his shoulder like a rake. It had been a nuisance all the way. There had been no detailed instructions with the map the Norns had given them – they were just told to make their way from the landing stage to the castle and slay the ogre. Ivo had longed for this adventure but now he thought that they must have been mad to set off so ill-equipped.

The Hag had brought a small holdall with the foot water, the magic beans and some underclothes for herself and Ivo.

Suddenly the troll stopped dead and pointed. An animal was peering at them through the bushes, staring with fierce and uncannily intelligent eyes. It was about the size of a badger but they could not make out its shape in the poor light. An air of menace came from it – and in a moment it had vanished.

They walked on wearily through the strange unpleasant wood. The path sloped slightly upward now but still there was no sign of a clearing.

'My goodness,' said the Hag, staring down at the ground. She was used to weird things that slithered about in the Dribble but the pale gigantic worm crawling across the path in front of them was like nothing she had ever seen. It was the size of a serpent but its body looked soft and wet and swollen, as though it had lived inside something warm and moist. The gut of an enormous animal, perhaps, or even . . . of a giant.

They trudged on silently. Ulf was looking grimly at the unhealthy trees; they badly needed thinning and dead branches littered the undergrowth. Trees were like people to him – he couldn't bear to see them badly treated.

After another hour, Ivo stopped.

'I can feel it,' he said. 'I can feel the castle.'

The others wanted to say that one cannot feel castles – but it was true that they too were aware of something looming towards them – and then the mist rolled away slightly and there it was.

*

46

It was exactly as they had seen it on the Norns' magic screen – enormous, with turrets and towers and places for pouring boiling oil – but no one was pouring oil or anything else. It had a deserted look, like the castle in Sleeping Beauty: silent, bewitched and sad.

'Well, we'd better get on with it,' said the troll.

They walked up a sloping meadow and across a drawbridge slung over a murky-looking moat. The chains were rusty, the boards creaked, but no one challenged them. Nor did anyone stop them as they passed through the gatehouse. A huge kennel stood beside the gate, but there was no sign of a guard dog.

Still in silence they walked across the courtyard – and stopped dead.

In front of them was a grating in the stone – and coming though the bars . . . was a hand.

It was a human hand, pale and desperate as it twisted and groped and searched. Now a second hand joined it, larger than the first, and then both hands twirled and searched and groped, their fingers frantically curling and uncurling on the iron bars. And as the rescuers stood with beating hearts they heard voices from below.

'Oh, when will it happen?' said the first voice.

'Is it my turn yet?' wailed the second.

'I cannot bear it,' moaned the first voice again. 'I cannot bear the waiting.'

And all the time the pallid hands groped and writhed like the tentacles of some imprisoned creature, searching for the light.

It was hard to move towards them but the rescuers forced themselves up to the grating and looked down.

Attached to the groping hands were people – a

47

man and a woman, no longer young. Their faces were turned upward and when they saw the rescuers their moans became louder and more pitiful.

'When?' they cried. 'When will our time come?'

'We must know.'

'You must tell him –'

The Hag's kind face was filled with pity. Ivo knelt down, peering into the dungeon which held the prisoners. Ulf was trying to prise open the grating, shaking it with his strong hands.

But before they could help the prisoners, they heard a noise which rooted them to the ground. It was a scream – a blood-curdling, hair-raising scream from inside the keep. And it sounded as though it came from someone young.

The rescuers turned and ran towards the noise. They raced up a winding stone staircase, along a corridor – and found themselves in the Great Hall of the castle. And there, incredibly, they saw exactly what the Norns had shown them on the screen.

A gigantic ogre with bloodstained teeth and glittering eyes was standing in front of the fireplace. He was roaring with rage, spittle came from his mouth and his enormous hairy fists were clenched, ready to shake or throttle the person who was kneeling before him. A young girl with long dark hair and pleading eyes.

'Please,' she implored. 'Please, oh please . . .'

But the slavering beast who loomed over her showed no mercy. He brushed away a cockroach, which had crawled out of his ear, and raised an arm the size of a tree trunk.

'No!' he roared. 'Be silent. Your pleas are useless.'

And he reached for his nail-studded club.

In the doorway the rescuers froze in horror. The Norns must have foreseen the future; the dreadful danger to the kneeling girl; her anguished pleas. This was the moment they had shown on the screen – the instant before the girl was destroyed.

They waited no longer. Ivo raised his sword, the troll grasped his rowanwood staff, the wizard mumbled his spells – and they rushed forward.

'Stop!' they cried. 'Stop at once! Let go of the princess!'

The ogre turned and saw them. And then an extraordinary thing happened. Over the monster's hideous face there spread a look of relief . . . of utter happiness. He dropped his club.

'Thank goodness you've come,' he said. 'It's a miracle! A minute later and I'd have been done for.'

And he sank back on to a claw-footed sofa and closed his eyes.

Ivo blinked and put down his sword. The troll lowered his staff. Everyone was completely bewildered.

'We've come to rescue the Princess Mirella,' Ivo said, looking down at the cowering figure, still on her knees.

And they waited for the grateful girl to rise and come towards them.

Mirella got to her feet. She took a deep breath – and then she let fly.

'How dare you come in here and interrupt? How dare you try to rescue me? I've been working on that wretched ogre for days, trying to make him do what I want – and just when I might be getting there, you come barging in.'

She stood on the bearskin rug and glared at them. Then she took the poker from the fire stand. 'If you come any closer I'll hit you,' she said as the rescuers stood and stared at her. 'I suppose my mother sent you. Well, don't come near me, that's all, or you'll be sorry.'

And she flounced out of the room and slammed the door.

The ogre had been lying limply on the sofa. Now he looked up.

'You'll have to take over,' he said. 'I absolutely can't go on and you can tell them so. I'm feeling very faint. And keep that dreadful girl away from me.'

And he slumped back on to the cushions with a weary groan.

Eight
Grief in the Palace

At first no one at the palace could believe that Mirella had gone. They were sure she was playing a trick on them, hiding somewhere close by, and they searched in all sorts of ridiculous places. Inside chests of drawers, or behind curtains, or in cooking pots. They called and whistled and begged and entreated her to come out from wherever she was, and her mother even offered to bring Squinter back if only Mirella stopped teasing them.

When this didn't work a proper hunt began. The police were called and scoured every inch of the palace grounds and went into every house in Waterfield, and the army were sent out to hunt in the surrounding countryside. The sound of bloodhounds baying could be heard all through the night, the school children were told to pray and sing hymns and people wept openly in the streets.

At first her parents had thought it might be a kidnap attempt and they waited every moment of every day for a ransom note but none came.

'She can't possibly have run away,' said her mother, 'not when she had everything a girl could want.'

So had she met with some dreadful accident? Wells and rivers were searched, the lifeguards put out to sea, the boy scouts looked in potholes and caves – but still day followed day and there was no sign of the princess.

Both her sisters were sent for – Sidony came with her husband who had brought his stamp collection to sort out while they waited, and Angeline came with her husband, who sucked even more peppermints when he was worried. Both the sisters were expecting babies and they sat and knitted baby clothes and shook their heads.

'Could she have run away to a travelling zoo or something?' Sidony wondered. 'She was so nutty about animals.'

But there hadn't been any travelling zoos or circuses in the neighbourhood for many months, and their mother always started to cry again when anyone suggested that Mirella had not been entirely happy at home.

After a week, as people began to think that Mirella might be dead, the school children were given a day's holiday, the flags flew at half mast and they could no longer put off giving the terrible news to Prince Umberto.

So Mirella's father went to Asmora where he found Prince Umberto in a mauve quilted dressing gown being measured for a new suit by his tailor while a hairdresser rubbed pomade into his hair . . .

The prince was very upset indeed to hear that his intended bride was missing and perhaps dead.

'Oh dear,' he said. 'This is terrible. Quite terrible.'

And indeed it was. Umberto owed money to his tailor and his shoemaker and to the man who trained his racehorses and he hadn't paid for his new carriage. Up to now he had kept everyone quiet by telling them that he was going to marry a princess whose father was very rich and who would pay all his debts – and now he didn't know what to do.

'I shall have to order some mourning clothes I suppose – fortunately black suits me – or is it too early? I mean, there may still be good news.'

But as the days passed there was no news at all. In the war, when someone disappeared, they put out bulletins saying, 'Missing: Presumed Dead'.

It was these words that the police now wrote in their files.

Nine

What Ogres Eat

The troll bent over the ogre who was lying limply on the sofa. His breath was shallow and when the troll levered up the ogre's huge wrist and felt his pulse, he found that it was far too fast.

'If you hurry, you can free those poor wretches down in the dungeon,' said Ulf quietly to the others, 'and then we can think what to do about the princess. I'll stay here and if it looks as though he's coming round I'll warn you.'

So the others hurried downstairs and across the courtyard, to the grating. There were no groping hands this time, but they could hear voices and the same wails as before.

'Hullo there,' called Ivo. 'We've come to help you! We're going to set you free. Do you know where the key is for the dungeon?'

A head appeared – it had thinning black hair combed over a bald patch and a drooping black moustache. A second head bobbed up beside it – that of a woman with a sharp nose and tight blue-rinsed curls.

'What key?' said the man.

'There isn't a key,' said the woman. 'You can get in if you go down the steps over there to the oak door. Just open it, it's not locked.'

'You mean you're not locked in?' The Hag was

54

completely bewildered. 'But then why don't you escape?'

But the heads had disappeared. The rescuers made their way to the steps and down to an oaken door. It was opened from the inside – and two people dashed towards them.

'Where is the ogre?' asked the woman with blue-rinsed hair.

'Do you bring news?' enquired the man with the sad moustache.

The dungeon was furnished in a rather unusual way. There was a sofa in one corner and a table with chairs in another. On the table were a large teapot, a plate of biscuits and a pack of playing cards.

'Yes we do,' said the Hag. 'We bring you wonderful news. The ogre is ill and he won't harm you – so you can go home. You're free. Only you must hurry, there's no time to waste.'

There was a moment of total silence, and then it began.

'Go home?' said the man. 'You must be mad. I can't go home – I've sold my house and my car to come here and I'm staying.'

'You mean *our* house and *our* car,' said the woman, glaring at him. 'And I've given up my job,' she went on, 'so we can't possibly go back.'

'I've never heard of anything so silly,' said the man, tugging at his moustache. 'Why would we want to go home after taking all the trouble to get here? If the ogre isn't feeling well enough today we'll just wait till he feels better.'

'Tell him we're not going home and no one has any right to make us,' said the woman. 'And tell the people in the kitchen that we've run out of teabags . . .'

The rescuers looked at each other. None of them could make head or tail of all this.

'We'd better go back upstairs and try to find out what's going on,' said the wizard.

They found the ogre propped up on cushions sipping something the troll had mixed for him.

'They won't go away,' said the Hag wearily. 'And they're not imprisoned, either.'

The ogre put down his cup. 'Did you say they won't go away?' he rumbled in his hoarse voice.

'That's right,' said the Hag. 'They said they couldn't go back to where they'd come from.'

'Did you tell them that I was finished? Through?' asked the ogre.

'Yes. Well, we told them you were ill.'

'Oh God – what have I done to deserve this,' said the ogre clutching his forehead.

But the rescuers had had enough. 'However ill you feel,' said the Hag firmly, 'you really must tell us what all this is about.'

There was a groan from the sofa.

'No, it's no good groaning,' the Hag went on. 'We've come a long way and nothing is what it seems. If you explain we may be able to help but not otherwise.'

The ogre looked at the troll hoping perhaps that he would be forbidden to excite himself, but Ulf too was looking at him and waiting. So the ogre gave one more deep groan – and then he began.

'You know what ogres do?' he said.

'They eat people?' suggested Ivo.

56

'Exactly so. But I never liked the taste of human flesh,' he said. 'The first time I ate a person it turned the corners of my mouth blue and gave me a pain here.' He put his hand on his side. 'It's my liver I think. The livers of ogres are very sensitive. I thought maybe he was too fresh – the bloke I ate – so after that they brought me an idiot who'd shot himself instead of the deer he was after but it wasn't any better.' The ogre shuddered. 'Ugh, I can taste him still.'

'My wife was alive then, a wonderful ogress. She didn't care what she ate – her grave is behind the castle – but she reminded me of my duty. Which was to be terrifying – to be ferocious . . . So I began to do what ogres have been doing for thousands of years. Next best thing to eating people was to change them into beasts. Turning human beings into animals. It was considered a dreadful punishment and quite right too. Anyone who came near I changed and when I ran low I sent my servants out to find more people. I turned the postman into a wolverine and the plumber into an okapi and the man who came to mend the roof into a worm. I was the best shape changer in Ostland and humans were terrified to come near me.

'Then my wife died. She was a wonderful woman,' said the ogre again. 'I wish you could have met her – the top of her legs measured twelve feet around and every square inch covered in long black hair.' He sighed and went on with his story. 'I rather let the castle go after that but I went on changing people – it was what she'd wanted.

'Then one day a truly awful thing happened. I'll never forget it. It was a Thursday. The last day on which a thing like that should have happened.'

'Because Thursday's Thor's day, isn't it?' put in Ivo. 'The God of Thunder. I saw it in the encyclopedia.'

'That's right,' said the ogre. 'I found a man trespassing near my wife's grave. Weedy little fellow. Well, I picked him up and brought him in and I told him I was going to turn him into a fish and throw him into the moat. A fish mind you – wet and dumb and slimy to hold. So I waited for him to scream and plead and beg me not to and do you know what he did?'

The ogre paused and searched them with his bloodshot eyes.

'He smiled,' said the ogre. 'I can see it now, that smile – and he said, "Oh yes, thank you, thank you. A fish would be so restful. I wonder . . . I suppose it couldn't be a gudgeon – they have such pretty fins."' The ogre paused. 'That's what he said. Those were his very words. I was so shocked, I did what he said – he's out there now in the moat. You can recognize him – he's got a look.

'And that was the beginning of the end. People came – more and more of them and asked me to turn them into animals. Said they were tired of being human, nothing worked – their jobs, their marriages . . . they'd thought of killing themselves and then they thought no, they'd rather go on living but as an animal.

'Since then I've been besieged. People come all the time and they won't take no for an answer. The place they're in used to be a perfectly good dungeon with torture instruments and hooks for hanging and they've turned it into a sort of club room, and sit there drinking tea. What's more, they come with lists of animals they want to be – not just a dog but a Mexican Hairless dog . . . not just a rabbit but an Angora rabbit with lop ears and spots . . .' The ogre's voice was getting higher and higher, and the troll poured a spoonful of medicine and gave it to him.

'Well, I can't eat them so I changed them – after all I am an ogre. And then along comes this girl – the Princess Mirella – and suddenly I couldn't take any more. A young beautiful girl – a princess – and she wants to be a bird. Can't face being a princess, can't face being married to the bloke her parents picked out for her. And not any bird – a white bird. I could tell her a thing or two about birds – if you want to see something really nasty watch two turtle doves having a fight. And I'm sick of it,' said the ogre. 'I'm turning into someone who's taking on the sins of the world – making life better for people who have mucked up the planet. Do you hear me? I'm making life better – and me an ogre.'

He tried to sit up, dreadfully agitated, and began to cough.

'I'm not being true to myself,' he spluttered. 'Ogres are fierce and wicked, they're here to do harm. So I told her I wouldn't do it and then . . . well, you saw her – tears, pleading, fuss. I tell you I'm through. No more changing, not ever.' He let his head roll back on to the cushion once more and closed his eyes. 'I need a rest,' he said. 'A long, long rest. I think I'm having a nervous breakdown.'

The troll now took charge. The sofa had castors and with all of them pushing they managed to wheel it into the ogre's bedroom and in a few minutes the ogre was lying back against the pillows of his enormous four-poster bed.

As they tiptoed out, his voice followed them. 'You'll have to stay and look after me,' he said. 'They're nasty things, these breakdowns. Very nasty indeed.'

Ten

Charlie

'Now what?' wondered the Hag.

They were all completely exhausted. If everything had gone according to plan they would now be dragging the body of the ogre away and setting Mirella free. Instead the troll was making medicine for him, and the princess they had come to rescue had locked herself into a room in the tower and wouldn't come out. Was there a punishment for failing their mission? If so, they were in trouble.

Ivo settled matters by yawning and the Hag made up her mind.

'We must all go to bed. Now. There are sure to be enough bedrooms in the castle. After a night's sleep we shall know what to do.'

So they went exploring – opening and shutting various doors. Some were store rooms and some were empty with clouds of dust rising up from them, but eventually they found a corridor with a number of doors which led into fairly ordinary bedchambers. The beds were enormous of course, as were the chairs and bedside tables, but the rescuers were too tired to care about details. The troll shared a bedroom with Ivo, not too far away from the ogre so that he could hear him if he called in the night; but the Hag and the wizard had rooms to themselves.

It was as he was undressing that the poor wizard

had a nasty shock. Undressing was always difficult for him – he so easily got tangled up in his trousers and he was holding on to the bedpost to keep his balance when he thought he saw, on the ceiling, the same floating face he had seen when they were crossing the sea.

Was it his mummy again, checking up on him? When he was a little boy she had often come in at bedtime to make sure that he was reading his *Book of Spells* and not the *Beano Annual* he had saved up for.

But when he looked again, he saw two spiders scuttling away and realized that the grey shape was the web they had been spinning, and with a sigh of relief, he climbed into bed.

Ivo slept heavily and at first he did not hear the scratching at the door. Ulf's bed was empty – he must have been tending the ogre – but he had left a candle so Ivo went to open the door, and in a minute the animal that stood outside ran past Ivo and took a flying leap on to his bed.

It was a small mongrel dog, white, with brown splodges on his back and ears, alert, intelligent eyes and whiskery eyebrows, and it was clear at once that he liked Ivo's bed, and liked Ivo. His tail went like a windmill, whimpers of pleasure came from his throat. He rolled over so that Ivo could scratch his stomach, and as Ivo scratched, he closed his eyes and helped him, moving one paw in rhythm with Ivo's hand, as kind dogs do.

'Where do you come from?' Ivo wondered.

But it didn't matter where he came from, Ivo was just incredibly pleased to see him. After all the fear and the strangeness, here was a warm, friendly living thing, and something ordinary.

The little dog yawned and burrowed into the pillow, setting it right for the night, and Ivo curled up beside him. He was just drifting off to sleep when it occurred to him that perhaps the dog was not so ordinary after all. Perhaps he was someone the ogre had changed and Ivo was going to spend the night hugging a headmaster or a tax inspector?

For a moment the thought was frightening – then he put it out if his mind. Whatever the little mongrel had once been, what he was now was a warm, breathing, loving dog – and Ivo's friend.

And while everyone in the castle was asleep something sinister happened down in the kitchens. The door opened and a procession of strange people in brown capes and hoods came out and set off across the drawbridge and down the path that led to the sea. They carried sacks filled with their working clothes, and with food that they had stolen. These were the ogre's servants who had finally decided to leave. They had been thinking about disappearing for a long time because everything was going to pieces in the castle since the ogress died, but it was the teabags that were the final straw. When a message came from the couple in the dungeon that they had run out, something just cracked in the cook. She said she was leaving and then all the other servants said they were leaving too.

So when the Hag woke in the morning and made her way down to the kitchen, she found it deserted. The great range was cold and there was scarcely any food to be seen.

She turned to find Ivo, who had left the troll asleep. Trotting behind him was the small white dog, who greeted the Hag enthusiastically, sniffing her shoes and wagging his tail.

'He's really nice,' said Ivo. 'I've called him Charlie.'

But it was what to do about breakfast that was the problem.

They hunted in the larder and found a piece of bacon that looked as though it might be edible, and a loaf of stale bread – and at least there was some coffee.

'I might as well be back in Whipple Road,' grumbled the Hag as she fried the bacon while Ivo put out the plates.

The other rescuers came in and ate breakfast too but it was clear that something had to be done. The ogre was bedridden, the dungeon was full of people who refused to go away and the princess was still shut in her room.

'I've saved some bacon for her but you'd better take it up,' said the Hag. 'She may be better with someone of her own age.'

Ivo took the tray, which contained a piece of bacon, a cup of coffee and a slice of toast. He decided to leave Charlie downstairs, which was difficult but the Hag diverted him with an old bone while Ivo slipped out.

As he toiled up the round stone stairs to the East Tower, he was remembering how he had felt when he first saw the Princess Mirella on the Norn's magic screen. She had looked so pathetic and terrified with her hair streaming down her back and her pitiful face and he had felt a great longing to save her and protect her – well, anybody would. And when he burst into the Great Hall, waving a sword which he saw at once would hardly scratch the ogre's backside, it was the thought of rescuing the princess which had given him the courage to go forward.

And all she had done was yell at him and threaten him with a poker. By the time he reached the top of the stairs, Ivo was in a thoroughly bad temper.

'Open the door,' he called. 'I've brought you your breakfast.'

There was no answer, but when he turned the iron ring in the door it creaked open slowly.

Mirella was lying in a huddled heap on a couch covered with a bearskin. The room was otherwise bare except for a broken spinning wheel, a battered leather footstool and a tool for dismembering things, nailed to the wall. Everything was covered in dust. She looked so forlorn that Ivo's bad temper subsided.

'I've brought you your breakfast,' he said.

Mirella raised her head. 'I don't want it.'

'Well, you'd better have it just the same.'

'All right. Put it down then.'

'I'm not your servant,' said Ivo, getting cross again. 'You might at least say please. And I think you're a ridiculous, spoilt brat. My goodness, when I think that I spent my whole life – my whole life – in a dreary boring Home eating disgusting food and being ordered about by bossy matrons and sharing a dormitory with people who sniffed and snored and played silly tricks on me, and you,' said Ivo, getting thoroughly worked up, 'you were brought up as a princess with everyone doing what you wanted and having lovely things to eat and clothes to wear, and you can't face the thought of going on living.

65

You have to run away and –'

But he was not allowed to finish. Mirella threw off her bearskin and sat up.

'How dare you talk to me like that! How dare you! You know absolutely nothing about being a princess. Well, let me tell you what it's like. You wake up in the morning with your room full of nurses and servants and people with lists of what you've got to do that day. You're put into ridiculous clothes and when you try to do anything interesting, it's forbidden. People throw away your ants' nest and –'

'Ants' nest? Did you have one of those?'

'Yes. The carpenter helped me make it. We lined it with plaster of Paris and the ants liked it and had very interesting lives, but my parents took it away. They took away my stickleback tank too and my jackdaws and everything I've ever loved, even my – ' She broke off and turned her head away. Talking about Squinter hurt too much. 'I was watched morning, noon and night and made to wear dresses covered in rosebuds and then this prince came and they said I had to marry him.'

'But you're much too young to get married,' said Ivo, quite shocked by this.

'They arrange these things early in royal families. He was completely horrible with a silly beard and a squeaky voice and a scented handkerchief which he waved when he saw anything alive – and he sleeps in bedsocks. One of his servants told my nurse. And then they took away my Squinter –'

Mirella's voice broke. She sniffed and wiped her eyes. 'The ogre has got to change me. He's absolutely got to.'

'Well, he can't,' said Ivo. 'He's having a nervous breakdown.'

Mirella frowned. 'I don't know what that is.'

'I didn't either but the troll told me. It's when you get so upset inside your head that everything sort of folds up – your blood and your digestion and your muscles. Nothing works properly and you become ill all over.'

'Well, he'll have to stop because I'm staying here till he changes me and that's it.'

'You're being very selfish.'

There was a scratching noise at the door. When Ivo opened it, Charlie came bounding into the room, full of good cheer and very certain of his welcome.

Ivo bent down to pat him, but Mirella had sat bolt upright and given a little shriek.

'Oh!' she cried. 'It's Squinter! It's my – ' Then as the dog came forward and she could see him in the light, her face fell. 'No it's not! His eyes are wrong.'

Ivo was indignant. 'What do you mean, his eyes are wrong? He's got lovely eyes.'

'Yes, I know. Oh . . . it doesn't matter.'

'Look, if you come downstairs we could share him. Please. There's so much to do.'

But seeing what she had thought was her beloved dog had reduced Mirella to a wreck. 'Just go away will you,' she said. 'And you can take the tray back too. I don't eat bacon, I'm a vegetarian.'

She managed to wait until the door was shut and then she threw herself on to the couch in a storm of sobbing.

Eleven
The Ogre's Breakdown

The ogre was not getting better – in fact he was getting worse. His thighs throbbed, his forehead pounded, blisters had come out on his stomach. At night he had terrible dreams and occasionally he screamed in his sleep – horrible screams which echoed through the castle.

'Oh, why did Germania have to die,' he moaned. 'It's all hopeless since Germania died.'

Germania was his wife, the ogress he had loved so much.

The troll did his best to nurse him but the ogre was not a good patient. He didn't like his medicine and he wouldn't get out of bed to do his exercises so he got weaker and weaker and he wouldn't let the troll bath him.

'Ogres don't have baths,' he said. 'It's not what they do.'

So a family of woodlice settled behind his ear, liking the warm dampness; leeches clung to his yellow toes; a spittle bug lived in his left nostril.

Everyone did their best. The Hag remembered a spell for bringing down swellings which she had used in the Dribble, but as soon as one part of the ogre subsided, another part swelled up again. The wizard mixed potion after potion but the ogre just turned his head away. The only thing he wanted them to do was sit by his bed and listen to his dreams, which were mostly about his aunts.

The ogre had three aunts who lived in separate places a long way away. There was the Aunt-with-the-Ears who could hear a man turning over in his bed on the other side of a mountain, and the Aunt-with-the-Nose who could smell people at a distance of twenty furlongs, and the Aunt-with-the-Eyes who could see an insect stirring in a neighbouring county.

But the rescuers were not only trying to look after the ogre. Every room in the castle was dirty and neglected, there was very little food and the couple in the dungeon only came out to ask for breakfast or lunch or dinner and went back in again.

'We'd better see what there is outside,' said Ulf.

So they went out over the drawbridge. In the moat they came across the gudgeon whom the ogre had changed. He seemed to be happy and contented though they couldn't be sure. Finding out what fish are thinking has never been easy.

On the other side of the bridge they found a walled kitchen garden and an orchard, both overgrown and full of weeds. There were a few vegetables still in the ground and the soil was good but there was a lot of work to do – and in the orchard rotten apples lay where they had fallen. They were on their way back when Charlie suddenly took off and, following him, they came to a large mound entirely covered in bare, gnawed bones. To their surprise Charlie did not pick up a single bone but sat down respectfully with a few quiet wags of his tail. Coming closer they saw that the mound was a grave and on top was a tombstone with the words: 'Here lies Germania Henbane of Oglefort, beloved ogress and wife of Dennis Consandine. Much Missed.'

'Oh dear,' said the Hag. 'That's another thing that needs doing. We'll have to tend the grave. Some of those bones look dreadfully untidy. Those grumblers down in the dungeon will have to come and help or go away. We can't do everything on our own.'

But the grumblers wouldn't help and they wouldn't go away. They turned out to be a married couple called Hilary and Neville Hummock and they had come to Ostland because they didn't like each other any more.

'In fact we hate each other,' Mrs Hummock had explained. 'So I'm going to be a wombat and live on land and Neville is going to be a mudskipper and live in the water and that way we won't see each other.'

Ivo thought he had never heard anything so silly – but it was Mirella that everyone was worried about. She hadn't eaten anything since they'd arrived and she was still shut up in her room. After all, they had come to rescue the princess and as far as they could see she was just fading away.

'I'll have one more go,' said Ivo. 'I don't know if it'll be any use but I'll try.'

This time he took Charlie straight away. Mirella didn't open the door at first but when the dog scratched at the wood, the handle turned slowly.

'What do you want?'

Ivo put down the tray. 'I want you to come down and help. I want you to be sensible. The Hag's working her fingers to the bone and those horrible people in the dungeon won't do anything and the ogre's taken to his bed and here you are just sulking.' He paused.

70

'Please, Mirella. Please? I thought maybe we could be friends – there isn't anyone else of my own age.'

But he was shocked by the way she looked. Her black eyes had rings under them, she seemed hardly to have slept, her hair was in tangles . . . If she wasn't ill already she soon would be and Charlie too seemed to be worried as he sniffed round her ankles and whimpered.

'It's no use. My parents will find me sooner or later. They're bound to. They'll send out armies and all that sort of stuff and when that happens I'll jump out of the window. I'd die rather than go back.'

'That's silly. You're just being a coward.'

'I am *not*!' Mirella rounded on him. 'I came over the bridge above the ravine in the dark and there were some ghastly creatures sort of moaning and gibbering and trying to get me, and then I walked for miles and miles without food and it was scary but I didn't mind because I thought when I got to the ogre he would change me into a bird and everything would be all right, but now I can't be bothered with anything.'

'And suppose he had changed you – perhaps it wouldn't be so marvellous. You'd have to eat things like ants which you kept as pets in the palace, and all sorts of insects.'

'No I wouldn't. I'd be a sea bird and swoop down into the waves.'

'Oh yes? I suppose spearing fish in your beak would be better? I suppose you think fish don't feel pain – you've seen them twitch and wiggle on the end of a line.'

Ivo was getting angry again. 'When I think of the

people who've been told they're ill and they're going to die – children even – and they'd give anything they've got –'

But he couldn't get through to Mirella. She had sunk into a black hole where nothing existed except her own despair.

'Isn't there anything we can do about her?' Ivo asked the Hag. 'How can she not want to be a human being . . . a person with arms and legs and *thoughts*? Why does she want to throw it all away?'

He looked out of the window at the brilliantly green grass, the clear blue sky. They had expected only darkness and danger but it was very beautiful at Oglefort. There was so much to learn and see and do, and he and Mirella could have done it together.

The Hag put an arm round his shoulder.

'Give her time,' she said.

But time was something that they didn't have. Mirella was quite simply dwindling away – and after a sleepless night Ivo took his courage in both hands and went to see the ogre.

What he was going to ask of him was difficult but he couldn't see what else there was to do.

Twelve
The Changing

Ivo had never spent any time in the ogre's bedroom – it was the troll who did the nursing. Now he waited till everybody was out of the way and crept up to the door.

From inside came a kind of heaving, juddering noise which grew to a climax, faded away – and began again. The ogre was snoring.

Ivo pushed open the door and walked in.

The ogre's bedroom was vast and grey and had a strange and rather unpleasant smell. The more the troll tried to get his patient to wash, the more the ogre said he did not hold with that kind of nonsense.

As his eyes got used to the gloom, Ivo noticed the medicine bottles by the bed, the spittoon for spitting into and the pile of torn up sheets which the troll had given him to use as handkerchiefs. On the ogre's warty nose, as it rose and fell, the spittle bug was taking an evening walk.

When he got up to the bed, Ivo coughed. Then he coughed harder. After Ivo's third cough, the ogre gave a great roar and sat up in bed. Still half asleep, he bared his teeth hungrily – then he remembered that he was no longer a flesh-eating ogre but a person with a nervous breakdown.

'What do you want, squirty boy?' he roared.

'Please, I need to speak with you about –'

But the ogre now remembered that he needed a lot of things, and that the troll had gone away with some nonsense about seeing to some trees.

'My pillow needs turning,' said the ogre, and lifted his head so that Ivo could manhandle the huge cushion full of chicken feathers. It was heavy and smelt of blood because the feathers it was stuffed with had not been cleaned.

'And I need some of that blue medicine,' said the ogre, pointing to a large bottle. 'Three spoonfuls. It's very nasty but if it wasn't it wouldn't do me any good.'

Ivo poured out the medicine.

'And I think I'd better have one of those pink pills in the saucer.'

When he had swallowed all these he lay back and said, 'Now that you're here, squirty boy, I'll tell you about my dream. It was about one of my aunts. The-Aunt-with-the-Ears we called her. You could have set up camp inside her ears they were so huge. Well, in this dream . . .'

The ogre was off and Ivo listened as well as he could. Dreams are not often interesting – they don't have a beginning, a middle and an end like proper stories, but he knew that people who have them usually want to tell you about them so he tried to be patient.

But when it was over and the ogre suggested that Ivo might give him another pill, he summoned up his courage.

'Please,' he said. 'I've got a favour to ask you. It's an important one. Very important.'

The ogre did not like the sound of this.

'I'm ill,' he said. He groaned a couple of times to make this clear. 'I'm having a nervous –'

'I know. But it's about Mirella, the princess. She's not eating anything and she just cries and I'm afraid she's going to get ill.'

'I'm ill,' said the ogre crossly. 'I'm very ill indeed. I'm ill all over.'

'Yes,' said Ivo, 'I'm sure you are. But about Mirella –'

'She should go home,' said the ogre. 'She ought to be glad I haven't eaten her and go back to her parents.'

'Well, she won't. She says she'd rather die and I think she really might. You see she had a sort of vision thing, a proper one like the saints used to on mountain tops. She saw these white birds on the roof of the palace and they were so free and above all the fuss and all she wants is to be like that too. Absolutely any white bird would do – well, perhaps not those owls that fly at night and bang into things but – oh you know – gulls and gannets and all those. Then she would fly off and she'd never bother you again.'

The ogre lifted his head from the pillow. 'Are you suggesting I change her?' he yelled. 'When you know that I have given up all that sort of thing for ever and ever – and that I am having a nervous breakdown. You must be out of your mind. Do you know how much force is needed even to change a hedgehog into a flea?'

'No. But –'

'Have a look at my left toe. See those swellings. And my stomach.'

He began to fumble with the bedclothes but Ivo did not feel up to the ogre's stomach and he handed him another pink pill and a green pill, which the ogre swallowed greedily.

'It wouldn't take long,' begged Ivo.

'NO. I absolutely refuse. Go away.'

Ivo stood up. Then he turned and said, 'You could do it in your dressing gown. You wouldn't even have to go out of the room. And your slippers.'

'NO!' yelled the ogre again.

He closed his eyes and pretended to snore. But Ivo stood his ground – the image of Mirella in a huddled heap wouldn't go out of his mind.

'If we didn't have to keep looking after the princess we could do important things,' he said, 'like tending your wife's grave. The bones are all over the place.'

'Oh, they are, are they?' The ogre didn't like this. 'Germania was very tidy.'

'We could get some unusual bones, maybe,' Ivo went on, 'and make an interesting pattern.'

'What sort of a pattern?'

'Something with skulls would be good. A sort of pyramid. We could make it look really nice. But it would take time and we can't leave the princess.'

The ogre shook his head. 'I can't do it, I'm too tired,' he said, and let his head fall back on the pillow again.

Ivo had reached the door when the ogre opened one eye.

'In my dressing gown and slippers, did you say?'

And Ivo said: 'Yes.'

The Changing was to take place in the Hall so as to give Mirella plenty of room to fly up and away but it had to be kept secret from the grumblers. There would have been a riot if they'd known that Mirella was to be changed and they weren't.

Ivo's face was streaked with tears. Though he and Mirella had quarrelled every time they met, he minded losing her more than he could have believed.

The Hag and the other rescuers were also very unhappy about what was to happen.

'I used to think it would be nice to be a frog when I lived in the Dribble,' said the Hag. 'Just plopping in and out of puddles . . . But it was only a fancy. This is too much magic, it's too strong.'

But what could they do when Mirella was determined to starve herself to death? So they assembled in the hall, waiting. The troll had strewn some pine needles on the floor of the platform where she was to stand; the Hag had picked a red rose for Mirella to hold while she still had hands.

Then Mirella came in. She had cleaned herself up as well as she could, rubbing her face with a wet cloth and shaking out her hair but she still looked rather a mess – and very small, dwarfed by the huge room.

Then the door opened and the troll, straining all his muscles, pushed in the ogre in a wheelchair, which his grandmother had used in her last days. He still wore his pyjamas and his legs were covered in a blanket made of moleskins which had been nibbled rather badly by mice.

Charlie, sitting at Ivo's feet, gave a whimper. The ogre put one foot on the ground and moaned.

'My back,' he moaned. 'The pain . . .'

But as no one took any notice he managed to stand up and stood there, swaying.

The Hag came forward and put the rose in Mirella's hand.

Mirella stood as though she was made of stone. If she was frightened she didn't show it. In a few minutes – a few seconds even – she would be flying over the heads of everyone. She looked round to see how she would get away afterwards and Ivo came up to her and said, 'I've left the window open – the round one above the banners,' and she whispered her thanks.

The ogre began to pass his hands back and forth over Mirella's head.

In the hall everyone held their breath.

Everyone except Charlie.

The little white dog had been watching, his piebald ears pricked, as the ogre bent over Mirella. Now for some reason he left Ivo, leaped on to the platform and ran up to her, yapping excitedly, and began to wag his tail and lick her feet.

Mirella bent down to him, 'It's all right, Charlie,' she said. 'Lie down. Be quiet.' And to Ivo she said, 'Call him off, can't you?'

'No, I can't,' said Ivo. 'He has a perfect right to say goodbye. He wants you to stroke him.'

'I know perfectly well what he wants,' snapped Mirella.

She had never touched Charlie before. Now as she felt his rough coat under her hand, his warm tongue licking her bare leg, something extraordinary happened to her. It was as though the scales fell from her eyes. She saw the Hag, so old and weary, who had trekked miles believing Mirella to be in danger. She saw the other rescuers – the troll and the wizard – and Ivo who had thought she might be his friend. Above all, she saw the living, warm, excited little dog.

And suddenly a feeling flooded through her – of thankfulness for being alive, of joy in the world. She looked up at the window through which in a few moments she would fly out and away forever, and felt panic, thinking of the loneliness that would follow.

But she had to go through with it now. She had suffered so much to get here, she had been so obstinate and determined – she couldn't change her mind now. She closed her eyes and lifted her head as the ogre's hand came down towards her.

The hand never reached her. The ogre gave a terrible cry, took two tottering paces forward and fell to the ground with a crash that echoed through the hall.

Everyone rushed forward, but the ogre could not move; he only pointed with his great arm to the doorway, where a figure as large and hideous as he was himself was standing, wreathed in a ghostly mist.

'Germania,' whispered the ogre – and fainted.

Thirteen

Removing the Grumblers

The ogre had bruised his forehead badly when he fainted at the sight of his wife. The Hag had found the foot water which the Norns had given them and it helped a little, but not very much.

'They must have been the wrong kind of feet,' said Ivo, who was beginning to have a very low opinion of the Norns.

But it was not the bruise that was worrying them; it was the ogre's state of mind. He had decided that Germania's ghost had appeared to him because the ogress wanted him to join her in her bone-covered mound.

'She has been hovering over me ever since she passed on,' said the ogre. 'I have felt her hover. A heavy hover, because she's a big woman. So I have to die. I have to die quickly so that she doesn't get impatient.'

The ogre having a breakdown had been bad – but the ogre deciding to die was worse.

'I can't stop eating at once, but I shall stop eating slowly, so every day you must weigh my food and take off an ounce. And I must decide which pyjamas to wear for the funeral and who to invite. My three aunts of course, and they'll have to bring Clarence.'

'Who's Clarence?' asked Ivo – but the ogre only shook his head and sighed.

'But you can't do this,' said the Hag. 'You've got a castle to care for – look at all the land out there and the gardens and the lake. What's going to happen to it?'

'I shall make a will,' said the ogre. 'Perhaps my Aunt-with-the-Eyes should have it – she's the eldest. Or the Aunt-with-the-Nose . . . Obviously I can't leave it to Clarence. It'll probably take a few weeks for me to be properly dead – I'll have decided by then.' He waved a lordly hand. 'And you can look after everything till then, can't you?'

The rescuers looked at each other. They thought that the ogre was getting a bit above himself.

'I have a house in London, you know,' said the Hag.

'And I have a job,' said the troll.

'My mother is waiting for me,' said the wizard.

But the truth was that 26 Whipple Road did not look very inviting from a distance. Mr Prendergast would be all right and after the way Gladys had behaved the Hag did not feel that she had to hurry back to her toad. And there was going to be a terrible row about Ivo whenever they got back. Nor did Ulf long to go back to pushing trolleys down hospital corridors. The ogre might be taking a lot for granted but actually no one was in a hurry to return.

'We'll look after things for a while,' said Ulf, 'but you must give up all thoughts of dying. It's a really silly idea.'

But the ogre just closed his eyes and said Germania was waiting for him. 'You'll have to make the mound bigger so we can both get in. And I'll need someone to write things down as they occur to me. I think my

81

mauve pyjamas would be best for the funeral but mauve's rather a sad colour. I don't want to depress people.'

The ogre had been dragged back to his bed, still muttering his wife's name, and was now in a deep sleep as Mirella joined the others in the kitchen. She was no longer the sulky obstinate girl who had shut herself in the tower but had straight away helped the Hag to prepare the lunch, and now she and Ivo were doing the washing up.

'I know how to get rid of the people in the dungeon,' said Mirella.

'How?' asked Ivo. 'How can you get rid of them?'

'I'll show you,' said Mirella. 'Come with me.'

With Charlie running at their heels, they made their way across the courtyard and knocked on the door of the dungeon.

'Have you brought us some lunch?' asked Mrs Hummock.

'No,' said Mirella. 'But we have some news from the ogre.'

The sulky pair came hurrying up to her.

'He's going to change us then?' asked Mr Hummock.

'At last, at last!' said his wife, clapping her hands. 'I knew he'd come round.'

Mirella put up her hand. 'Well, yes – but there's something he'd like you to do first.'

'And what is that?' asked Mr Hummock.

'Well, you see the ogre is feeling very weak. That is why he hasn't changed you up to now. But he feels sure that if he had one particular thing to drink – and lots of it – he'd get better very quickly.'

'And what is that?' asked Mrs Hummock.

Mirella paused. Then she said dramatically: 'Blood!'

There was a moment of silence.

Then: 'What kind of blood?' asked Mrs Hummock.

'Human blood. It must be human blood and he needs lots of it. Not just a few pints like one gives in a hospital, but buckets of it. He says if you'd allow yourselves to be completely drained he could drink enough blood from you to get up his strength for the changing. Of course you'd be almost dead – just white wraiths really – but it wouldn't matter because the next moment you'd be whatever you want to be. It hurts rather as you'd expect – there's a special syringe that goes into you and it just sucks and sucks – you can see your muscles turning paler and paler and your skin going blue, but the ogre is sure you won't mind. He's sending someone down first thing tomorrow morning to do it. You'll need a good knife to make a cut in the flesh for the nozzle to go in and –'

'All right, all right, we get the idea,' said Mrs Hummock.

'Are you going to do it too?' the husband asked Mirella. 'Give your blood?'

'Of course. I'm a princess – I'm not afraid of pain,' said Mirella grandly. 'Well, we'll see you later. The ogre said there's no need to tidy up down here because there's always a bit of leakage and the blood gets everywhere so the whole place will have to be swilled out afterwards.'

She waved cheerfully and left the dungeon.

'Do you think it'll work?' asked Ivo.

'It'll work, you'll see,' said Mirella.

The Hag was a little shocked when she found out what Mirella had done but that didn't stop her going to the kitchen window several times an hour to see if anything was happening. There was no movement all that afternoon and when they went to bed the grumblers were still there. But in the morning, when they made their way cautiously to the grating, the dungeon was empty.

And now at last, with the ogre in bed and the grumblers gone, the rescuers could set to work outside.

As they crossed the drawbridge they could see the lie of the land. To the west was a dark line of trees at which the troll stared longingly, and the blue glimmer of a lake. To the east the ground was flat, a kind of marshland stretching away to the sea. But straight ahead of them, past Germania's burial mound, was the walled garden and the orchard, and it was the garden that they were heading for. The Hag carried a trug and Ulf trundled a wheelbarrow full of tools. The wizard was sitting with the ogre, but the children ran ahead with Charlie; it was wonderful to be out in the open.

The kitchen garden must have been a marvellous place before the ogre had let everything go to seed, but now the great yellow marrows and swollen cucumbers were over-ripe and rotten and the creepers had run riot. What had been a strawberry bed was just a mass of mouldy straw with a few red splodges where the berries had fallen to the ground.

'All the same the soil is excellent,' said the Hag. 'If one had the labour one could grow anything.'

They set to work, digging up those vegetables that one could still eat, wheelbarrowing the rotten ones away to the compost heap. Along a wall of old bricks grew peaches and apricots – some were mildewed but some could be used, and the children found a stepladder in the tool shed and started to pick them.

They worked for a couple of hours. The sun was hot on their backs but there was a tap in the wall where they could drink when they got thirsty.

'I'm going to go and look in the orchard,' said the Hag when she had squirted water over her shoes. 'I'm sure there will be some windfalls we can use.'

The troll followed her but the children stayed, picking blackberries from a bush which grew over the cold frames.

'Look, here's another door,' said Mirella, pushing back a creeper which covered the wall.

They pushed it open and found they were in a second garden – mostly full of long grass. There was a trellis covered in rambling roses along one wall and there were a few rose bushes with dark red blooms in a border. An old greenhouse stood in the corner; two of the windows were broken and the roof looked as though it would collapse at any minute. They were about to go back when a volley of excited barks from Charlie made them turn. He was standing at the door of the greenhouse, his coat bristling, his nose quivering with excitement.

'What's the matter, Charlie?' asked Ivo.

Charlie's barks grew louder. The children hushed him and went to look in at the open door.

Lying on a heap of sacking, lifting his great head sleepily, was an enormous creature like an outsize antelope. Two curved horns came from the side of his head, large yellow eyes stared at them. A tufted beard hung down from his face, and he did not seem to be at all pleased to be disturbed.

'What is it?' whispered Ivo.

'It's a gnu,' breathed Mirella. 'A kind of wildebeest. There was one in the zoo at home.'

For a moment the children just stared. Gnus are strange-looking beasts at the best of times. They belong on the African savannah, moving in herds between their watering holes. To see one a few feet away lying on the floor of an old greenhouse was incredible.

The gnu gazed at them in silence. Then he rose and stalked away over the grass.

Two days later the children were in the orchard picking the last of the apples. Ivo was holding the ladder and Mirella was reaching up for the ripe fruit. The Hag had taken a wheelbarrow of windfalls up to the kitchen.

'They'll make excellent jam,' she'd said contentedly. She had lived through the war when everyone grew their own food and knew there is nothing better than that.

The children went on working. It was very peaceful; wasps droned over the fallen fruit, the sun shone. They were moving the ladder to another tree when there was a sudden eerie cry – a wail of fear it sounded like, high-pitched and shrill – and looking up they saw a dark creature, about the size of a small cat, bounding along one of the branches. For a second it turned and looked at them, then it fled, leaping away towards a stand of tall oaks which sheltered the orchard. They only had time to make out two enormous yellow eyes with black rings round them, a pair of naked ears and a long bushy tail.

'Is it a lemur?' wondered Ivo.

Mirella shook her head. 'The tail's wrong. Lemurs' tails are striped. I think it's an aye-aye,' she said excitedly. 'They come from the rain forests of Madagascar – usually you only see them at night. Oh, this is so amazing – I've always wanted to live among animals – it's like being in Paradise.'

Over lunch in the big kitchen, Dr Brainsweller told them more about these mysterious little beasts.

'The people who live in the rain forest are very superstitious about them – there are all sorts of legends. Some of the tribes believe they carry the souls of the dead up to heaven,' he said. 'We're very lucky to have one here. I knew a wizard who'd have given his right arm for a hair from an aye-aye's head – he wanted it for a spell to raise his dead grandmother from her grave. Not at all the thing to do of course but he had set his heart on it.'

Though they were working harder than they had ever done in their lives, the children had never been so happy. Ivo was right when he'd thought that he and Mirella might become friends; already they seemed to read each other's minds. It was great to be doing really useful things, picking fruit, digging, clearing ditches, instead of sitting at their desks learning stuff they would probably never need. The adults too loved working out of doors – but they had their work cut out looking after the ogre.

'Are you making my mound bigger?' he wanted

to know. 'Must be able to get in comfortably beside Germania.'

He had decided against wearing the mauve pyjamas for the funeral.

'Say what you like, mauve is a sad colour. Melancholy – I think the striped pyjamas would be best.'

And he'd changed his mind about which aunt he was going to leave the castle to.

'I think the Aunt-with-the-Eyes should have it,' he said. 'She's the oldest, so I think it would be fair. I shall expect you to witness my will when I've written it. And I shall need a hearse.'

'A hearse takes people to the graveyard for burial, doesn't it?' asked Ivo. 'And you're only going to go as far as the mound.'

'All the same, I want everything to be done properly. There's a cart in the shed. You only have to build it up and paint it black and put my name on it. And a skull and crossbones perhaps.'

So that was another job for the rescuers to do.

They saw the gnu several times; he did not seem at all bothered by their presence – but the aye-aye was dreadfully shy. They heard its thin eerie screech and a couple of times they were close enough to see its strange fingers – thin and long like the fingers of a witch – as it dug in the bark looking for grubs, but it never came down from the trees.

The aye-aye was not the last of their discoveries.

The glimmer of blue they had seen when they first crossed the drawbridge turned out to be a beautiful lake, large and silent, with water lilies covering the surface. In the middle of the lake was a flat rock, the kind that mermaids used to sit on and comb their hair.

Then one day, after a hard morning's weeding and digging, Ivo and Mirella went down to the water to cool off. They sat under an overhanging willow and dabbled their feet in the water. They were just wondering whether to plunge in and have a proper swim when there was a great swirl on the surface of the lake and then slowly a head came above the surface. In the head were two round piggy eyes and a huge mouth, which opened to show vast pink gums.

As they watched, the animal pulled itself slowly and laboriously out of the water and heaved itself on to the rock – where it stood for a moment yawning and shaking itself and looking about.

It was a hippopotamus. Not a full-sized beast but a pygmy hippo about the size of a small cow but with all the characteristics of its bigger brethren. Its hide was smooth and shiny in the sunlight, and it looked very clean and appetising. A piece of water weed hung from the side of its mouth and it gazed at the children for a long moment, before it slid into the water once again.

Fourteen

The Hag Finds Her Dribble

But it was not only the unusual animals that were to be found in the ogre's enchanted gardens. After they had worked steadily all week the Hag said she thought they should have Sunday off and explore the surrounding countryside.

When they had crossed the drawbridge they all went their separate ways. The troll went off towards the line of trees in the distance; the children followed the stream which fed the lake to see where it led; the wizard wandered along the hedgerows looking for interesting plants for his potions. But the Hag went east, to where the flat ground stretched towards the sea.

She walked on, watching the cloud shadows scudding across the fields. She was worrying about Ivo. He seemed to have settled in to life in the ogre's castle as though he had been born to it, but of course they couldn't stay here forever. The ogre would get better and if the worst happened and he didn't, then his relatives would come and take over. And she simply could not face taking Ivo back to the Riverdene Home. Would they let her adopt him? Almost certainly not. They were more likely to put her in prison for having abducted him.

She had been so busy worrying that she had not looked carefully enough at the ground. Now she found that she was walking on marshy land. Her shoes were beginning to sink into the soil and make a squelchy noise.

The Hag became alert and excited. She looked down at the plants: bog myrtle and cotton grass and asphodel – she knew them all. Now the ground was getting wetter and wetter; the squelchy noise made by her shoes was getting louder. Then a frog plopped up in front of her and disappeared into a puddle. A puddle that was almost a pool. She knew it all so well, the way a puddle could become a pool and a pool become a puddle. She knew the dragonflies that hovered over them, the water boatmen scurrying about on the surface. She looked up at the sky, which was reflected in the still water and saw the swarm of midges which hovered above her head. Now, as she made her way between a clump of bulrushes, the water was almost over the top of her shoes. Almost, but not quite. Because she was not walking in a lake or a drain or a ditch. She would not sink completely – there would always be enough soil to hold her weight.

The Hag made her way to a boulder sticking out over the surrounding marsh and sat down. She was suddenly overcome with joy. As she sat there quietly she could feel the wetness seep up her stockings and reach her knickers . . . then the bottom of her vest . . . she closed her eyes, blissfully remembering.

'Oh, thank you, God,' said the Hag. 'Thank you.'

Here in this far off place she had found what she had never hoped to see again.

A Dribble.

*

It was not only the Hag who had found her heart's desire. Making his way to the distant line of trees, the troll had found a forest as rich and varied as the woods of his homeland.

'There's a lot of work to be done there of course,' he said, when he and the Hag met again on the bridge on their way back. 'The trees need thinning out, old wood has to be cut away – but it's a real forest, not silly rows of Christmas trees waiting to be felled. If only my brother were still alive . . . There's an oak there that must be five hundred years old.' He shook his head sadly. Here was man's work, work for a lifetime, not wheeling trolleys up and down hospital corridors. 'Well, it can't be helped,' he went on, 'we've got a few weeks so we'd better make the most of them.'

Dr Brainsweller was in the garden, picking interesting herbs which might be useful for magic potions, and thinking about his childhood. It seemed to him that he had not really had much of a childhood at all. When he was a little boy he had wanted to be like other children – he did not feel called to wizardry and magic in any way – but his mother had put him in for every single wizardry competition and had got him the best tutors in the dark arts that she could find.

But now, as he bent down and gathered up a bunch of dandelion leaves, he couldn't help thinking that it had not really been worthwhile. In his workshop at Whipple Road he had tried to make gold from ordinary metal and all that had happened was that he had burned a hole in the ceiling. He had tried to concoct an elixir which would make people live forever and it had only given the people he tried it on a stomach ache. And anyway, thought the wizard, bending down to pick a bunch of chives, was it really a good idea that people should live forever and get creaking bones and have to have hearing aids in their ears which whistled and honked?

And he had to admit that he had been a failure as a warrior. When they charged into the Great Hall, meaning to slay the ogre, he had been muttering every spell he could think of for destroying things – the smiting spell, the thrusting spell, the spell to make a man drop dead – and it hadn't seemed to make the slightest difference.

Was he doing the right thing with his life? Not that it mattered – there wasn't anything else he could do.

He had come upon a patch of spring onions behind the broken greenhouse, and though he had never used spring onions in a potion before, he thought they looked rather nice. Then he plucked a young shoot from a vine, and found a radish under a broken cloche.

The radish, with its bright red colouring, cheered up his little bunch, and he returned to the kitchen to try and see what he could do. Since he no longer had a workshop he had taken over a corner of the kitchen and he went there now, fetched a wooden bowl and started to mix up what he had found.

He was turning the leaves over and over when he realized that it had happened again. There was a sound like the soughing of the wind and then as the mist cleared, he saw it. His mother's face was looking down on him – and her expression was one of horror.

'Bri-Bri, what are you *doing*?' she began.

'You're supposed to be a *wizard*.'

And then this odd thing happened again. Two very large spiders came hurrying across the ceiling and, as they did so, their webs swung out from a rafter and completely covered Mrs Brainsweller's face in a mass of cobwebby lace. She could be heard getting fainter and fainter and then she gave up, and her long worried face and spectacles disappeared.

The wizard looked up, meaning to thank the spiders, but they had already scuttled away, leaving the webs hanging on the rafter.

When the Hag returned she found Dr Brainsweller staring down at a bowl full of mixed leaves, and looking very shaken.

'What is it, Brian?' she asked him. 'You look upset.'

The wizard explained, and the Hag, who was feeling uplifted after her time in the Dribble, did her best to comfort him.

'She's just worried about you,' she said. 'Mothers are like that.'

The wizard sighed. 'I'm afraid I'm a disappointment to her.' He looked down at the contents of the bowl, which he was stirring absently. 'You can't blame her for being worried. I mean, it doesn't look much like a magic potion, does it?' he said sadly.

The Hag looked. She looked again. She fetched a bottle of olive oil from the larder and a bottle of vinegar. She fetched a fork . . .

Her face was shining. 'No,' she said. 'You're right. You haven't made a magic potion, Brian, but you have made something much, much better. You have made a salad!'

And from that day, the wizard did more and more of the cooking. He learnt to make excellent soup from the vegetables in the garden – because after all soup is not so different from a magic potion, it's all about stirring and mixing and sometimes a little muttering, and he tried out other recipes. He took great pride in the job and was happy for the first time in his life. And Mrs Brainsweller stopped appearing to him because the kind spiders always blotted her out with their webs and gradually she gave up and left her son alone.

So the wizard was happy and so was the troll – and the Hag was in a state of bliss because she knew that the Dribble was *there* even on days when she couldn't get to it.

As for the children, they couldn't imagine a better life than the one they now had.

Fifteen
The Ogre's Bath

When they had been at the castle for nearly three weeks they saw a man in a jerkin come over the drawbridge carrying a large churn of frothy milk which he wanted to sell them. His name was Brod and he kept a cow and some chickens in a smallholding on the other side of the ogre's land. He used to supply the ogre with milk and eggs in the old days but the ogre's servants had cheated him so badly that he'd stopped coming.

'But I saw them skiving off,' he said. 'So if you give me a fair price I'll do business with you.'

The Hag was delighted but worried too. 'I don't think we have any money,' she said.

Brod stared at her. 'The ogre's got a pile of gold pieces. Keeps them in his sock. You go and ask him and tell him it's Brod. He knows me.'

The ogre was not at all pleased to be interrupted, but he admitted that he knew Brod and said that they could look in his sock drawer for the gold pieces.

The drawer was not a pleasant place, but after a long search they found the gold coins and took one down to Brod.

'I'll supply you for six months for that,' he said when he had bitten it to make sure it was genuine.

So now they had milk and eggs, and the larder was filling with blackberries and dried mushrooms and they picked sloes and rosehips in the hedgerows.

'What an idiot I was wanting to be a bird up in the cold sky,' said Mirella. 'No trees, no grass, no water, no work to do – just empty space.'

But the ogre was beginning . . . to be a worry. At first they simply waited for him to give up the idea of dying, but he wouldn't. And if you get an idea like that into your head you can seriously make yourself weaker and weaker. He was also getting not just ordinarily disgusting, but very disgusting indeed. And there came a morning when they all stood around his bed and told him that he had to have a bath.

'Ogres don't have baths, I've told you,' he said. 'I never had one when Germania was alive.'

But Ulf said that if he wanted them to go on looking after him, a bath was essential, otherwise he was on his own. 'And anyway your aunts are coming. And Clarence.'

'Ah yes, Clarence.'

They waited for the ogre to tell them more about Clarence but he just sighed as he always did when he mentioned that name – and the moment passed.

'And you must change your pyjamas,' said the Hag. 'Leave those outside the door and I'll take them to be washed.'

Since the ogre could not fit into an ordinary bathtub except in bits, they decided to sluice him down in the laundry room near the dungeon where there were two huge copper vats which were used for boiling clothes, and a stone floor covered in wooden slats so there would be no trouble with flooding.

'But we must make sure that the insects which are

97

living on him are safe,' said Mirella. 'They'd die in all that water and steam.'

So she fetched all the jam jars and containers she could find and started to scoop out the woodlice from behind the ogre's ears and the spittle bugs from his nostril and the leeches between his toes. The ogre lay very quiet while this was going on because it put off the evil moment when he had to get up and have his bath.

'What about the bed bugs,' he said. 'Don't forget those.'

But at last every single creature was safely stored and labelled and the dreaded event could be put off no longer.

Ulf meanwhile had lit the fire in the range and dragged two enormous copper cauldrons out into the centre of the room, and scrubbed them clean. He had placed a stool between the tubs and found a rack for the ogre's towels, and laid out a long-handled brush and some soap neatly as he had seen the nurses do in the hospital, and added a large pot scourer and some caustic soda to be on the safe side. Then he climbed back up the stairs and started to get the ogre out of bed, which was a terrible business. The room had to be cleared because he was shy and as soon as he was standing upright and Ulf tried to help him on with his dressing gown, he sat down again, panting horribly and clutching his heart.

'You'll kill me before I've got my funeral sorted,' he said. 'And I've told you, ogres are better when they smell.'

'Ogres may be but we aren't,' said Ulf, who was longing to get out into the forest. 'Come on.'

Slowly – very slowly – grumbling furiously, collapsing again and again on the stairs, the ogre arrived in the laundry room. Clouds of steam were rising from the hot tubs and he gave a bellow of rage.

'You're going to boil me alive,' he roared. 'It's a plot.'

Ulf took no notice. He took the ogre's dressing gown and hung it on a hook. Then he poured two more buckets of warm water into the first of the gigantic tubs and the whole room filled with steam.

'Get in,' he said.

'Very well,' said the ogre. 'You are hurrying me on to my death but nobody cares. Germania would have cared, but she's under the mound.'

Ulf waited.

Still grumbling, the ogre began to lower his bulk into the tub. Water slopped on to the floor. Ulf picked up his long-handled back scrubber and the cake of soap. The ogre, complaining the whole time, lowered himself further, and then a little further still into the water . . .

The children had gone into the orchard to pick the last of the apple crop, when Mirella said suddenly, 'Oh no! I'm an idiot – the poor little bat – it'll be boiled alive in the heat.'

Ivo stared at her.

'What are you talking about?'

'The fruit bat in the laundry room – don't you remember? The very young one that was hanging above the range. I bet Ulf won't have had time to collect it and let it out.'

She ran like the wind towards the castle, and threw

open the door of the laundry room. Clouds of steam billowed towards her, the fire roared. She could make out nothing at first, then saw what she had expected.

The little bat had fallen to the ground and was fluttering, stunned and frightened, in a corner, half drowned, getting caught on the wooden slats. Ignoring everything except the animal she had come to save, Mirella knelt down on the floor, groping and searching. As soon as she had fastened her hand round the petrified, quivering creature, it squealed and bit and managed to free itself. Her clothes were soaked, her hair trailed in the puddles but she saw nothing except the plight of the terrified bat.

The ogre had lowered himself further into the tub – but as his behind touched the water, he rose up again, pointing a furious finger at Ulf.

'It's too hot! I told you it was too hot. You're trying to kill me.' He grabbed a towel and wrapped himself in it. It was only now that he saw Mirella crawling on the floor.

'And WHAT IS THAT?' he roared, wrapping himself tighter in the towel. 'Get it out! Get it out at once!'

Mirella neither saw nor heard him. She went on crawling along the soaking floor, her hand stretched out towards the trapped bat, while the ogre yelled and cursed, and more and more steam billowed through the over-heated room . . .

Sixteen

The Norns

After they had sent the rescuers off to save Princess Mirella and slay the ogre, the Norns fell in to a deep sleep. They slept for days and days, snoring gently in their bed in the cave deep under Aldington Crescent underground station.

And while they slept the ghosts went round and round in the ghost train along the deserted track, and the harpies roosted and the rats scuttled about, and water dripped from the roof.

When at last they woke, the Norns were very woozy, not quite certain where they were and how much time had passed. They sat up slowly and stretched out their skinny arms and the nurses who had been dozing in the back of the cave came forward with syringes and gave them injections, and handfuls of pills which they popped into their mouths.

Even so it was a few more days before the Norns remembered about the princess and the ogre. Then the First Norn said:

'Ogre slain?'

And the Second Norn said: 'And princess saved?'

'Must be,' said the Third.

All the same, they thought they had better make sure. The magic screen was brought down in the lift by the Norns' attendants and set up in a corner of the cave. Then the Norns were wheeled over, the necessary words were said – and the screen flickered into life.

As before, the picture showed the wave-lashed cliffs, then the forest path which led to the castle – then the castle itself.

There were no ogres to be seen in the great rooms of the castle – perhaps the monster was already dead and buried? And no sign of the rescuers either.

But now the picture travelled down and down, into the dungeon and past it – into a dreadful torture chamber full of smoke.

The smoke swirled and rose and blotted out what was in the room. They could make out nothing at first; there was only the smoke . . . or was it mist . . . or steam?

Then the hellish vapour cleared for a moment and they saw a truly terrifying sight. The hideous ogre, far from dead, was standing beside a boiling cauldron. He was wrapped in a kind of shroud, his fiendish face was twisted with rage, his great forefinger pointed at something which crawled like a tortured beast of burden on the floor.

At first they could not make out what this apparition was – then to their horror they saw that it was the Princess Mirella! The princess in sodden, filthy clothes, too terrified to rise to her feet, grovelling like the lowliest animal . . . They could not make out what the ogre was saying but his contorted face and the pitiless pointing finger made it certain that he was pronouncing her doom.

The screen went dark and the Norns, in their rumpled bed, became extremely agitated.

'Princess must be saved,' said the First Norn.

'And ogre slain,' said the Second.

'Slain utterly,' said the Third.

But that wasn't all. Something had to be done about the rescuers who had failed so spectacularly in their mission.

'Rescuers must be punished,' said the First Norn.

'Pulverized,' said the Second.

'Obsquatulated,' said the Third.

But who could they send? They had tried to find proper warriors at the Meeting of Unusual Creatures and they had failed. Too frail to leave their beds, the Norns peered hopelessly at the empty platform.

The ghost train went past. The white-faced spectres stared blankly in front of them. Water dripped from the roof.

'Who?' said the First Norn.

'Yes, who?' said the Second.

When a princess is in danger, something has to be done. This is a rule which binds all Unusual Creatures.

They went on swallowing pills, shaking their wobbly heads.

The ghost train came round again and still nothing occurred to them. Their eyes were beginning to close. What they wanted desperately was to sleep and sleep and sleep . . . With a great effort they shook themselves awake. The ghost train came in sight for a third time.

The Norns looked at each other. They struggled to their knees. They stretched out their bony arms.

'Stop!' ordered the First Norn as the train drew level with the mouth of the cave.

'Stop!' said the Second Norn.

'Stop absolutely!' demanded the Third.

The train slowed down, stopped. The door opened

a crack, opened a little further, opened completely –
and the spectres' white dead faces stared out
in puzzlement.

The ghosts in the train were not there for nothing.
The sins they were being punished for by circling
the circle line for ever and ever all had to do with
travelling.

Now they were bewildered. The train had never
stopped before – it just went round and round.

But it had stopped.

And the doors never opened.

But they had opened . . . they were sliding slowly
apart. And, not quite believing it, the spectres glided
out on to the platform.

There was the Honker – a very old ghost with one
leg and a crutch who had done nothing when he was
alive but honk and spit and let out huge revolting
gobbets of saliva which got on the seats and the floor
of the train for other passengers to slip on.

There was a ghost in city clothes and a bowler hat
who had sharpened the point of his umbrella like a
rapier and stuck it into the feet of any passenger who
got in the train ahead of its owner. The umbrella still
had bits of skin and blood clinging to it.

Behind him came the Aunt Pusher – a bruiser of
a ghost with great hands like coal scuttles. He had
pushed his aunt off the platform and under a train
because he wanted her money but when her will was
read he found that she had left everything to a Lost
Dogs Home, and after that he went mad and started
pushing everyone under trains who looked like his
aunt and wore a hat with feathers.

Two women ghosts glided out next. The Bag Lady was a fat ghost wearing a flannel nightdress and carrying a number of bulging carrier bags. During the war she had sheltered in the underground to get away from the bombs but instead of lying quietly on the platform like the other shelterers, she had spread out a whole lot of clothes and blankets and pretended she had a family who was coming, and had kept the other people away. Once she had turned away a young couple and they had gone back up the staircase and been caught by the blast from a bomb and been badly hurt.

The Smoking Girl was a very young ghost hung all over with gaudy scarves and floating shawls, and she would have been pretty except that her fingers and the corners of her mouth were stained yellow with nicotine. She had smoked a hundred cigarettes a day, coughing and blowing smoke at the other passengers on purpose. There was nothing she liked better than breathing her poisonous fumes into other people's lungs.

There was even a headless ghost, the Chewer, whose head was so stuck up with chewing gum that he had left it on the train.

But there was one more ghost to come! He came slowly, and at first he was only a grey wavery shape – a space, a nothingness. But what a nothingness! A cold and hopeless emptiness; a pit of such pointlessness and despair and fear that those who came near felt that life had no sense or meaning.

'The Inspector!' whispered the other ghosts, and stood back to let him pass.

The wavery shape became more distinct. It was the

figure of a man in a uniform with shiny buttons, the merciless dazzle of which pierced the eyes – and in his hand a ticket puncher with which he had punched the tickets of the passengers who were on the train.

But no face. Only two eyes, narrowed to slits, and a mouth set in a slimy calculating leer. The Inspector had had power over the spectres when they were alive, turning off passengers whose tickets were not in order, pushing them out on to the line, separating mothers from children, making sure that trains stuck in tunnels for hours – and always talking about 'the regulations' to justify his cruellest deeds. His creepily soft call of 'Tickets please' had sent shivers down their backs and even now they were afraid of him.

The Inspector seldom spoke. He did not need to. His ticket puncher, which once had pierced paper, could now pierce ectoplasm.

The Norns looked at the ghosts and were pleased with what they saw. The ghosts were deeply disgusting. Ectoplasmic spit is probably the nastiest substance there is and the Honker had just produced a gobbet of it, which landed in the lap of one of the nurses. The Bag Lady's phantom knickers had risen from one of her carrier bags and were drifting round the cave looking for a victim. All the garments in her carriers could wrap themselves round people's faces so that they couldn't see.

But that wasn't what pleased the Norns. An ogre might not be scared of ghosts that were just disgusting. He himself was probably disgusting too. No, what was terrifying about these ghosts was the sheer evil and selfishness that seemed to hang over them like a black mist. There is nothing more frightening than spectres who have lived with cruelty and viciousness day after day, and even the Norns, used as they were to strangeness, found themselves shivering. One murderous deed may be forgiven but these ghosts had practised evil morning, noon and night.

'Ogre must be killed,' began the First Norn.

'Ogre of Oglefort,' said the Second Norn.

'Killed absolutely. Finished,' said the Third.

'Frightened to death,' said the First Norn.

'Terrorized,' said the Second.

'Pulverized,' said the Third.

'And the rescuers must be punished,' said the First Norn.

'Horribly.'

'Cruelly.'

'Shouldn't be difficult,' said the Aunt Pusher, smiling his horrible smile. 'Ogres are afraid of ghosts, everyone knows that.'

'What about our reward?' asked the Ghost with the Umbrella. 'What do we get if we do the job?'

The Norns blinked at each other. They were not used to rewarding people – but the ghosts just stared with their relentless eyes.

Then: 'Train will be re-routed,' said the First Norn.

'Not just round and round,' said the Second.

'Different stations,' said the Third.

'Junctions,' said the First Norn.

'Branch lines,' said the Second.

'Tunnels,' said the Third.

The ghosts were satisfied, nodding their horrible heads.

'How do we get to Oglefort?' asked the Bag Lady.

'Orders will be given,' said the First Norn.

'Instructions,' said the Second Norn.

'Information,' said the Third.

The Norns were now exhausted. The nurses came forward with syringes to give them an injection but nothing could stop the Old Ones from falling asleep. One by one their heads fell forward on to their chests, they slid down under the bedclothes . . . they began to snore. And the ghosts glided back on to the platform and into the train and sat staring out of the window at the dark tunnel – and waited.

Seventeen

The Magic Beans

The children and Charlie had followed the stream which led from the lake. They had taken off their shoes and socks and were treading carefully over the bright sharp pebbles. Charlie was not content with paddling. He plunged into the water, swam across to the other bank and back, shook himself all over them, and plunged in again. He waited with his head on one side while they threw sticks for him, and more sticks and more sticks still, and after that he began a ferocious tug of war with a tree root, growling like a werewolf. But whatever he was doing he came back to them, sneezing with pleasure and sharing his happiness. He was a great believer in sharing.

'I thought I'd never love a dog after Squinter, but I was wrong,' said Mirella.

'He makes everything seem as though it's just been invented, doesn't he?' said Ivo. 'I mean, look at him with that stick – you'd think there'd never been a stick like it in the whole world.'

The little dog still slept on Ivo's bed, but as soon as he woke in the morning he trotted off to see Mirella who now had a bedroom along the corridor, and when the children were apart he simply went backwards and forwards between them.

'He'd never let us quarrel,' said Mirella.

But the children had no wish to quarrel. They

agreed exactly about what they wanted to do: make the castle gardens grow, stock the larder, tend the land. And perhaps – though they did not put this into words – turn the place into somewhere where people would not want to be changed but would be content to be themselves.

'If only we had more help,' said Ivo, as they made their way back to the castle. 'The kitchen garden needs digging all over and the rose garden needs mulching and Ulf says we ought to be pruning the trees in the orchard. And the Hag gets so tired.'

'Yes I know. Maybe the animals could help. People used to use animals on farms.'

'But not hippos or gnus or aye-ayes.'

'No . . . but why not? The gnu could pull a cart; it takes ages to wheelbarrow the stuff to the compost. And the hippo could help us to find out what's going on in the lake. Catching fish would be a big help.'

'We could ask the ogre a bit more about who the animals were – the gnu and the rest. He might remember.'

But the ogre said he couldn't remember anything like that and anyway he was far too busy with the arrangements for the funeral.

'I've changed my will again,' he told them. 'I'm going to leave the castle to the Aunt-with-the-Ears. I've thought about it and I think she'll do better than the Aunt-with-the-Eyes. She dances you know. She goes round and round when you play a waltz and her teeth flash, and I think it will be jolly when I'm under the mound to have a dancing aunt about the place, don't you agree? And what about

110

the hearse, how is that getting on?'

He had also changed pyjamas again. Not the ones he was wearing, which were turning a rather messy grey colour, but the ones he was going to be buried in.

'I think they should be my silk ones. I shan't be cold if I'm beside Germania. Oh, and there's the music for the funeral. I think I want a brass band with lots of trombones – I've always been fond of trombones.'

So it was no good trying to get help from the ogre. But in the night Ivo woke and remembered something which made him sit bolt upright, and disturb Charlie who was not at all pleased.

The Norns had given them three presents before they set off on their quest. The sword had been useless, and the foot water hadn't been much good either. So probably the magic beans, which would make whoever ate them understand the language of the animals, would turn out to be useless too.

But not necessarily – and as soon as it got light he ran along to Mirella's room.

'It's worth a try,' she said. 'Do you want to tell the others?'

'I don't think so. The Hag will only worry – she'll think we shouldn't swallow anything that hasn't been tried. I know where the beans are – in the holdall she keeps under her bed.'

'Good. Let's go for it then,' said Mirella.

The beans in the leather pouch looked small and black and . . . well, like beans.

'I suppose we'll have to eat one each and at the same time, if we're both to understand what the animals are saying,' said Ivo.

So they took two beans and put the pouch back in the holdall and then they shut Charlie in the kitchen and made their way out of the castle towards the walled garden.

They had decided to talk to the gnu first – and they found him in his usual place, dozing in the greenhouse.

'Well, here goes,' said Ivo. He held the enamel mug under the tap in the wall and swallowed his bean and Mirella swallowed hers.

Then they waited.

'Nothing's happening,' said Mirella. And then. 'No wait. I feel sort of . . . fizzy. No, more light headed.'

'And my ears are buzzing a bit,' said Ivo.

They walked over to where the gnu was lying. Then both together they said: 'Good morning.'

The gnu opened his yellow eyes and stared at them. He began to squeal and grunt – and then quite suddenly the grunts turned into: 'And good morning to you.'

It was an amazing moment. Each word was perfectly clear to them. They could even make out the Scottish accent in which he spoke.

'Could we ask your name?' said Mirella, sounding every inch a princess.

'Certainly,' said the antelope. 'I'm Hamish MacLaren. And who might you be?'

'I'm Mirella and this is Ivo. You'll have seen us about.'

'Yes, indeed,' said the gnu, 'but it is strange that I can understand you suddenly – and you can understand me. Why is this?'

'We've eaten some magic beans,' explained Ivo.

And because the gnu sounded so reliable and sensible they told him of all their adventures, the illness of the ogre and what they hoped to do in the gardens and grounds

And in return, the gnu, in his deep, steady, Scottish voice, told them his story.

He had been brought up in the Highlands, the youngest of four brothers. His parents died when he was small and he went to live with his grandfather in his stately home. The older brothers fitted in well – they liked doing all the things that Scottish aristocrats did – hunting and shooting and fishing.

'But I couldn't take to it,' said Hamish. 'The whole place smelt of blood: dead pheasants hanging in the larder, carcasses brought in on litters, dead fish with glazed eyes . . .

'I wanted to be an astronomer. I love stars, don't you?' said the gnu, looking up at the sky. 'But I wasn't clever enough. So I just had to help my grandfather, which meant bullying the tenants and killing things all day long.

'The house was full of the stuffed heads of animals that my grandfather had shot. There was a bison and a buffalo and a whole lot of stags; they had such nice glass eyes. My favourite was the gnu – he was in my bedroom and at night when I couldn't sleep I would talk to him. Then one day a traveller from Ostland came to see us and he told us about an ogre who turned people into animals. My grandfather didn't believe it but I thought anything would be better than living there, and having to shoot animals that I liked a hundred times better than I liked my relatives. So I sold my father's gold watch and took a boat to

113

Ostland, and found my way here. I knew exactly what animal I wanted to be and . . . well, here I am, and I have no regrets.'

When Hamish stopped speaking, everything in the garden seemed very quiet.

They could hear a bird singing in the orchard but it didn't seem to be saying anything.

Then they plunged into what they wanted to ask him.

'You see we so much want to make this garden really grow. And we were wondering if – whether you might help us. The Hag is very old and . . . well, there aren't many of us. Would you consider maybe pulling a cart . . . or grazing bits of lawn that we can't get round to cutting or . . . anything like that?'

The gnu was silent and for a moment the children were worried in case they had offended him. After all a Scottish laird might not want to work as a gardener.

But the gnu was nodding his great head. 'I'd be delighted to help,' he said. 'To be honest the time does go rather slowly when one is just sleeping or eating – and I'm quite strong. Pulling a cart would be nothing . . . or mulching a vegetable bed. Just tell me what you want me to do.'

'What a nice person,' said Mirella when they left the gnu. 'He couldn't have been more helpful.'

They had no idea how long the effect of the beans would last and as the aye-aye was nowhere to be seen they hurried down to the lake to talk to the hippo.

They walked round the edge, peering into the water, but it was some time before the creature's piggy eyes appeared above the surface.

'Please could you come a bit closer so that we can talk to you?' called Ivo.

The hippo stopped in the middle of a yawn and looked up, surprised.

'Would you tell us your name? I'm Mirella and this is Ivo.'

There was another long pause and the children were worried that the effect of the beans had worn off. Then in a deep voice with a northern accent, the hippo said: 'Bessie. I'm Bessie.'

She said it in a resigned sort of way as though being Bessie wasn't a particularly good thing to be, but she didn't sound unfriendly, just tired.

'How long have you lived here in the lake?' asked Ivo.

Bessie lifted her great head and opened her mouth. This seemed to be her way of thinking.

'A long time,' she said at last.

'Do you like it here?'

'Yes, I like it.' Bessie spoke slowly but they thought this was nothing to do with being a hippo. It was more that she had been a rather slow and dozy person.

Getting her to tell her story took much longer than learning about the gnu, but after a while the children pieced together her life before she came to Oglefort.

Bessie had lived in a small house in a drab industrial town. Her husband had left her with four children who seemed to be able to do nothing for themselves. Bessie cooked and shopped and mopped up after them, then when the children were grown up they brought their own babies back to the dark little house and it all started again: the screams, the mess, the nappies.

'The only time I had any peace was in the bath,' said Bessie. 'I would lock myself in the bathroom and run the water up to my neck. Even then they hammered on the door – but while I was in there I was happy.'

Then one day she took some of her grandchildren to the zoo. The children whined and grizzled and Bessie's legs swelled and her feet ached, and all the animals seemed to be miles away behind trees.

But then they came to an enclosure with a pool and there – walking slowly out of the water, was a pygmy hippopotamus.

'I just fell in love,' said Bessie now. 'It was so clean and so smooth and it didn't mind being fat – it just wallowed and swam and wallowed again.'

Her grandchildren had tugged, and whined for ice cream, but Bessie didn't move. She had found the perfect way of living.

Finding the ogre and getting him to change her had taken a long time. She consulted every book she could find on magic and the lore of changing . . . but at last she had heard about the Ogre of Oglefort.

'So here I am,' said the hippo. 'And I can't imagine how I stuck being human for so long.'

The children realized that she had come to the castle because she was tired and would not want to do much work towards restoring the grounds. But they knew she would be able to help them with one question.

'You see we need to find things we can eat and of course fishing is an obvious thing to do. But we don't want to eat – you know – changed people. A bank manager fried in batter probably wouldn't taste very nice and anyway there are things I suppose one just doesn't do,' said Mirella.

116

Bessie saw this entirely but she said there wasn't much need to worry. 'There's a pair of carp you want to steer clear of. They used to be philosophy lecturers in a university and spend the time worrying about how many angels can stand on the point of a needle and rubbish like that. I got to know them when we were waiting to be changed. But there's a lot of fresh water crayfish – you could fish for those – they're probably good eating. And the perch are just what they seem – not much flavour in them but if you're short . . .'

The children thanked her. 'You've been most helpful. We wouldn't be depriving you?'

'Dear me no. I'm a strict vegetarian.' She seemed to be thinking for a while. Then she said, 'I mostly came here to rest, but if you like I could clear the odd drain for you – there's a lot of weed choking some of the runnels. Just say the word.'

They found the aye-aye in the topmost branches of a bent fir and for a long time it wouldn't come down, just gave that sad high-pitched screeching wail which had seemed meaningless when they first heard it – but now they could make out what the terrified creature was saying.

'What do you want? Leave me alone. Don't hurt me.'

'We're not going to hurt you. We wouldn't dream of it,' said Ivo. 'We just want to make friends.'

It took a long time to coax the aye-aye down from the tree, and to hear her story, but when they did, they understood why she was so shy and seemed so unhappy.

117

'My name is Nandi,' the little creature said, staring at them out of her huge black-ringed eyes. 'I was born in India and they said I was pretty so from when I was a little girl my mother put me in for beauty competitions till in the end I was Miss India with a big crown on my head and a lot of fruit round my neck and everyone shouting. And then I was Miss Eurasia with pomegranates and a purple bikini and cameras clicking. Then when we came to England I had to be Miss Hackney South with a Union Jack on my bosom and a wand. And then they put me in for the Miss Universe competition but the heel came off my shoe in the procession and I fell over and everyone laughed – and my boyfriend was angry and left me because he had bet a lot of money on me winning. And he was the apple of my eye so my heart was broken and I came here and asked to be an aye-aye and live where nobody can hurt me.'

When Nandi had finished speaking in her breathless little voice the children were very shaken. They could see all the other contestants laughing and sneering as she ran off the platform, and they would have liked to put a bullet through the cruel man who had left her. They were so upset that they hardly dared ask Nandi if she would help them to make the castle gardens flourish but she already knew what they wanted.

'I will help pull down the fruit from the high branches,' she said. 'And I can put back some of the tiles on the roof. I have seen you working and I will help – but there must be no cruel men – and no competitions.'

*

118

'What nice people, they all seem to have been,' said Mirella as they made their way back. 'And all of them willing to help. After the grumblers I was expecting the worst.'

But as they got closer to the castle, they both fell silent, because they were absolutely dreading what they had to do next: talk to Charlie, and find out what kind of a human being he had been.

'Even if we tried not to,' said Ivo, 'I suppose it wouldn't work. Now that we've swallowed the beans we can't *not* talk to him.'

'It'll probably be all right,' said Mirella. 'He can't have been anybody really horrid – he just can't.'

They tried to think what sort of a person they wouldn't mind him having been.

'I suppose if he'd been one of those people who go bird watching and hiking at the weekends. Maybe takes school parties and shows them things?'

'In an anorak, with binoculars, who tells you it's not a lesser spotted flycatcher, it's a greater one?'

'Or a geologist with a little hammer banging at rocks?'

But though those sort of people do a lot of good in the world, they didn't want Charlie to be like that, and they didn't want him to be an out-of-work actor, or an office clerk whose boss had been unkind to him. In fact, they couldn't think of a single sort of person they really wanted Charlie to be and their steps got slower and slower as they got nearer home.

But when they walked into kitchen, the Hag told them that Ulf had taken the little dog to the forest and probably wouldn't be back for a while. The evenings were long and light and there was still no sign of Charlie or Ulf at the time they usually went to bed. Ivo went to his room and Mirella was just saying goodnight when there was a scratching at the door and when they opened it Charlie rushed into the room – tired, happy, muddy and ready to share his busy day in the forest.

The children looked at one another. Time to begin. So far Charlie's barks had sounded as they always did but it had been the same with the others at first – the gnu's grunts and the aye-aye's screeches had taken a moment to become understandable as human speech.

'Charlie,' said Mirella very seriously, taking the plunge and looking into the dog's eyes, 'we're able to understand the language of animals now so would you tell us who you are? Or rather who you used to be.'

And they waited, holding their breath.

But whoever Charlie had been, it was obviously not someone very quick on the uptake. He wriggled free of Mirella's grasp and began to play his favourite game, leaping over the footstool and waiting for them to catch him.

'Please, Charlie,' said Mirella. 'Speak to us. Tell us about your past. We have to know.'

Charlie rolled on his back and let his paws go limp, ready to have his tummy tickled.

But the children felt they had to go through with it now – and how could they scratch the stomach of someone who might presently tell them that he was a high court judge.

'Charlie, please try,' Mirella begged again.

But it was no use, and now Charlie had jumped on

to the bed and begun his evening rearrangement of Ivo's pillows.

'Of course,' said Ivo suddenly. 'I know what's gone wrong! All those magic things usually stop working after the sun has gone down. And it has gone down – look – there's not a ray to be seen.'

Mirella ran to the window, and it was true. The evening star had just risen on a darkening sky.

'We'll have to wait till the morning,' said Ivo.

The relief was tremendous. Neither of the children had admitted how frightened they were of hearing Charlie's story.

So Mirella said goodnight and went to her room, but as she passed the open door of Dr Brainsweller's bedroom, Mirella heard voices.

'Ridiculous person,' said a woman's voice, 'appearing like that and calling him Bri-Bri – and those absurd spectacles. No wonder the poor man gets upset – you did quite right, spinning a web over her face. We'll have to keep an eye on him – wizards are highly strung, everyone knows that.'

Mirella looked in at the open door. At first she thought the room was empty. Then she looked up at the ceiling where two large spiders were sitting close together, and conversing.

Mirella hurried on. She had understood the spiders quite clearly. So what on earth was the matter with the little dog?

She decided to wait till the morning, but as soon as it was light she crept back to Ivo's room and told him what had happened.

'So it wasn't that the beans had stopped working because I understood the spiders as clear as anything.'

121

They couldn't make it out. They tried again, asking Charlie simple questions, talking clearly and slowly – but all he did was scratch at the door and indicate that it was time he went out for his morning run.

'We'll have to go and see the ogre,' said Mirella. 'And I don't care if he's in a state about his funeral pyjamas or the trombones – we'll make him tell us who Charlie was. Now we've started we can't just stop.'

So they went to see the ogre who was just finishing his breakfast. They explained about the beans and the animals and demanded to know the truth about Charlie.

The ogre wrinkled his vast forehead.

'Charlie?' he said. 'Who's he?'

'The little white dog. The one who follows us everywhere. You must know who he is. White with a brown patch behind his ear.'

'Oh him,' said the ogre. 'He's a mongrel. Been around for a while.'

'Yes, but who was he?' said Mirella urgently. 'Who was he before you changed him?'

The ogre shrugged. 'He wasn't anybody. He's just a dog, always has been. Now about the hearse – I think it should have my name on the side, and a little poem. The kind you get on gravestones . . .'

But the children weren't listening. They were hugging each other, then dancing round the room – and Mirella's eyes had filled with tears of relief and happiness.

Charlie was a dog. Charlie was himself and nothing else. Charlie was Charlie!

Eighteen
Mustering Princes

The grumblers who had fled from the dungeon were on their way back home. They had managed to get a fishing boat to take them to the port of Osterhaven and were waiting for the overnight ferry bound for Great Britain, when Mr Hummock pointed to a notice on the harbour wall.

'My goodness, look!' he said. 'It's that wretched girl who tried to get ahead of us with the ogre and told us about the blood and the syringes and all that. The Princess Mirella.'

His wife came to look and sure enough, there was Mirella with her thin face and her wild dark hair. But it was what was written underneath the notice that really excited them.

REWARD it said in huge letters, and then: A hundred thousand pounds is offered to anyone who can give information about the whereabouts of the princess. Please apply to the Major Domo, Montefino Palace, Waterfield.

The couple turned to each other excitedly.

'That's a lot of money,' said Mr Hummock. 'Why don't I go to Waterfield and claim it and then I can send you your share.'

But his wife thought that this was a bad idea. They had decided to get a divorce and live in different places. 'I don't trust you,' she said.

So they agreed to go together and instead of boarding the ferry, which was going back to Britain, they waited for the local boat, which puttered round the island and ended its journey at Waterfield Docks.

'There are two people who say they have news of the Princess Mirella, Your Majesty,' said the Major Domo.

Mirella's mother leaped to her feet and called for her husband.

'Show them in quickly, quickly,' she said.

The Hummocks appeared. Both of them wanted to be the one to break the news, so they talked together and interrupted each other – but in the end Mirella's parents understood that their daughter was in the castle of the dreaded Ogre of Oglefort and in great danger.

'Oh heavens!' said the Queen, clutching her heart. 'Oh how dreadful – oh my poor dear girl!'

'We must send an army to rescue her at once,' said the King. 'There is no time to be lost.'

So the grumblers were sent off to get their reward and the King and Queen set to work to organize an army to slay the ogre and rescue their daughter from the evil monster's clutches.

'Philippe must bring his soldiers,' said the King.

Philippe was the prince with the stamp collection, the one who had married their eldest daughter, Sidony.

'And Tomas must bring some of his troops,' said his wife.

Tomas was the prince who sucked peppermints because he worried about his breath and was married to their second daughter, Angeline.

124

'But of course it is Umberto who must be at the head of the whole army,' agreed the King and Queen. 'And there is no time to lose.'

So messengers were sent to Prince Philippe and Prince Tomas, and to Prince Umberto – who was after all Mirella's proposed bridegroom.

The princes were not at all pleased. None of them wanted to confront an ogre, and their wives cried dreadfully.

Sidony cried because she was expecting a baby, and she begged her husband to stay at home.

'What if poor little Sweetie Pie was to grow up without a father?' she asked.

Angeline cried even harder because she wasn't just expecting one baby, she was expecting twins.

'I couldn't bring up the Little Puddings all by myself,' she sobbed. 'I simply couldn't.'

But of course they knew really that their husbands had to do their duty.

The most difficult to persuade was Prince Umberto, who had never in his life led an army or done anything braver than throw a wooden ball at a coconut, but he had no choice. He now owed so much money that without Mirella's father to bail him out he would have to flee his country or risk imprisonment, so he hurried to Waterfield in a very grand uniform and chose the most valuable horse in the royal stables for his mount – and to the sound of a splendid brass band, the three princes rode off to rescue Mirella from the vile and dreadful ogre who had her in his power.

The army which set forth looked impressive, though in truth it was composed mainly of friends of the princes and their servants. There were the

Household Guards in gold and purple with white plumes in their helmets, and the Royal Fusiliers in green and yellow with velvet caps, and the Soldiers of the Bedchamber in crimson and velvet. True, none of them had ever been in a battle, and there was a serious shortage of weapons and ammunition, but the people who cheered and waved and shouted as the army marched away were not upset by this. The school children were given a holiday and that night there was feasting and rejoicing in the town because everyone was certain that the ogre would be slain and the Princess Mirella returned to them.

Nineteen
Whipple Road

When Ivo was not returned to the Children's Home on the day he was due back, the Principal sent round the orphanage secretary to investigate.

The Secretary banged on the door in Whipple Road but nobody came. Mr Prendergast was at work and Gladys was under her stone in the back yard. In any case, even in her heyday when she was properly magical, Gladys had never been able to open doors.

So the Secretary went away and came back the next day and the next but still she got no answer. By now the Principal was worried. It was true that Ivo was only one of eighty-seven boys in the Home and she'd never noticed him particularly, but that wasn't the point. A child in her care was missing and something had to be done about it.

So, after working hours, she came back with the Secretary and this time they found Mr Prendergast at home. The enchantress and the henkies had moved in with friends but kind Mr Prendergast had stayed to look after the house.

'I'm afraid they have gone on a mission,' he explained, 'and the boy is with them. I've been expecting them back every day but there has been no sign of them.'

The Principal was absolutely outraged. 'They had

absolutely no right to take Ivo,' she said. 'It amounts to kidnapping.'

At this point Mrs Brainsweller, who had seen the orphanage van, came running in from two doors down with her hair flying and said her son too had disappeared.

'I managed to keep contact with him until a few days ago but now he's been blotted out,' she said. 'Absolutely blotted! There's a horrid grey mist over his face.'

So the Principal of the Orphanage, who obviously thought that Mrs Brainsweller's son was a little boy too, went to the police, and they put up posters with very strange descriptions of the Hag and the troll (but no photographs because neither of them would ever have their pictures taken). The notice was headed: CHILD SNATCHERS, and underneath it said: Have you seen these people? If so do not approach them – they are highly dangerous – but contact your nearest police station immediately.

There was also a very smudged photograph of Ivo taken on a school picnic with thirty other children and an arrow that said: The Missing Boy. (Actually the arrow was pointing to a boy called Bernard Sloope, but this is the kind of thing that happens in school photographs.)

But nobody came forward, so Ivo was put on the Missing Persons Register. Nor was there a reward for anyone coming to the police with information, because he was only an orphan and not a prince.

Twenty
The Ogre's Aunts

Ivo and Mirella had soon worked out that the magic beans, like all the Norns' gifts, were a little faulty: they only worked on animals who had once been humans. But this was useful in a way, for once all the rescuers had eaten the beans they knew exactly which fish they should eat and which animals might help them in their work.

The spiders who had protected Dr Brainsweller from his mother were two middle-aged sisters who had been turned out of their home by a greedy landlord. They had been very fond of knitting and thought being spiders might suit them – and there was a hedgehog who used to be a shop assistant in a department store and only wanted to be alone.

Most of the animals in the castle, though, were just what they seemed. The spittle bug in the ogre's nostril was simply a spittle bug. The woodlice in his ears were simply woodlice and the bats in the rafters were bats.

But the children's new friends in the garden were wonderfully helpful. The gnu made seed furrows with his cloven hooves, the aye-aye tied in the young shoots on the vines and Bessie began work on clearing the moat. Soon the grounds began to look really well tended and tidy, and everyone was proud of this because it seemed that visitors might soon come to the castle.

The ogre's bath had ended better than it began, but it was not long before he became restless again and said that he could feel himself becoming weaker by the hour and it was time to send off the invitations to the aunts for his funeral. He still hadn't quite decided which aunt to leave the castle to, and if they came a few days early it would help him to make up his mind.

'Once I see them in the flesh I shall know,' he said.

So he sent a messenger to the three aunts asking them to come, and he told them they could bring Clarence if they had nobody to leave him with.

The messenger he used was not a magical person but a cousin of Brod's, the man who brought the milk. This cousin rode round the countryside on an old grey horse and though he was not speedy he was reliable.

The messenger went first to the Aunt-with-the-Nose.

This aunt lived in a huge, dark cave – a cavern really. She was very pale because of living in the dark, but her swollen nose glowed slightly, which helped her to sniff her way about. She wandered around in the cave, smelling everything that lived down there: roots, earth, stones – and of course feet when anybody came to visit. She could even smell crystals and stalactites.

This aunt was a vegetarian: she ate roots and leaves and her hobby was worm collecting. She collected them because they did not smell in the way that furry animals do, and were no bother. She had the best worm collection in Norland and sometimes she swapped worms with other collectors or took them to worm shows.

When she got the message about the funeral, she came out of her cave, nose first, and shuddered a little because the scent of the grass and the trees and the flowers always overwhelmed her, they were so strong. Then she set off down the hillside, up another hill and down again until she came to the house of her sister, the Aunt-with-the-Ears.

The Aunt-with-the-Ears was waiting for her because she had heard her sister's footsteps as soon as she'd left her cave. She was a giantess, with ears the size of footballs, which drooped down on either side of her face. Her home was an old abbey with a carp pond which had been lived in by monks and she kept to the inner rooms so that as little noise came to her as possible, but she also had outsize earplugs made from old footballs. Even so, sometimes the sound of the rain plopping into the pond gave her a headache.

'Have you had your invitation from Dennis?' asked the Aunt-with-the-Nose.

Her sister nodded. 'He seems to think he's dying,' she said.

She wasn't particularly upset because ogres don't go in for family feeling. All the same, she thought they had better go.

'He says we can bring Clarence if we want to,' said the Aunt-with-the-Nose. 'We could put him on a trolley.'

'Yes, we'd better do that. I don't want to leave him – he just might be ready.'

The Aunt-with-the-Ears did not collect worms; she

collected eggs. She collected every sort of egg and because Norland was an unusual place she collected some very unusual eggs. Some of these had hatched into ordinary birds or reptiles, some had hatched into phoenixes or small dragons, and flown away.

But Clarence hadn't hatched. He was by far the largest egg that any of the aunts had seen – and though eggs can't really keep on growing it seemed to them that Clarence inside his egg was somehow forcing the shell outward without breaking it.

He had been with them for six years and still hadn't made his way out into the world, yet they were certain that he wasn't dead. Sometimes noises came from him – not cheepings, not cluckings, but . . . sighs; slight groans as though Clarence would have liked to get round to hatching, but couldn't quite make the effort.

So now they put him on his special trolley and covered him with his egg cosy to stop him from getting chilled, and wheeled him round to the third aunt, the Aunt-with-the-Eyes.

This aunt lived on the top of a tall tower which had once been a lighthouse. It was right at the edge of the sea and when the aunt stood and looked out with her great eyes she could see every ship within hundreds of miles. She too collected things but not worms or eggs – she collected the bones of sailors who had drowned. She gathered them up and bleached them and kept them in a special room in the tower: toe bones and ankle bones and thigh bones and ribs. This aunt was very thin because of running up and down the stairs of her tower. The Aunt-with-the-Ears was very tall and the Aunt-with-the-Nose was very portly.

And when everything had been settled, the aunts set off, pulling Clarence behind them on his trolley.

'After all Dennis is our nephew,' they told each other. 'And we'll have to see what's to become of the castle.'

'Yes, that's true. Who is he going to leave the castle to?'

They wondered about this all the way to Oglefort. The castle was the biggest and most important in the area – it must go to someone who mattered. And of course it should be someone from within the family.

If Clarence had only hatched and become someone remarkable, perhaps he would have had a chance to inherit – but the aunts were sensible women and they realized that the ogre couldn't leave his castle to an egg.

Twenty-One
The Battle

'Oh, when will the aunts come,' said the ogre in a weak and trembling voice. 'I feel terrible. I'm sure I can't last much longer.'

'You said it would take them at least a week to make the journey,' said Ulf. But he was getting worried. If the ogre died before it was decided which aunt was going to inherit the castle it would make a nasty muddle.

He felt the ogre's pulse, which was indeed extremely feeble.

'Try a spoonful of this – just a small one,' said the troll, reaching for a plate of gruel which the Hag had made, but the ogre only turned his head away and sighed.

It was at this moment that the gnu, out in the garden, lifted his great head. His ears twitched; he rose to his feet.

'What is it?' asked Ivo.

The gnu was looking anxious. 'I hear something,' he said. 'Keep very still.'

The children did as they were told. At first they could hear nothing – antelopes have much more sensitive hearing than humans. But as they waited and listened they too heard it.

Hoof beats. A large number of them. Horses were approaching the castle.

The gnu pawed the ground – ready to run off.

But at that moment the aye-aye came bounding through the branches and dropped to the ground beside them. Her eyes were wide with terror.

'There are men with uniforms riding towards us. I could see them coming over the hill. Many men – a whole army.' She began to whimper. 'Men like that are bad – very bad. They have flags with many colours – green and yellow and blue, and foolish hats. When men have such silly clothes they are dangerous.'

'Oh heavens!' Mirella had put her hands over her mouth. 'Those are my parents' colours – they have them on the royal standard. They'll have sent an army to fetch me away but I won't go – I won't go.'

'The drawbridge,' said Ivo. 'We must pull up the drawbridge.'

The children ran as fast as their legs would carry them into the castle.

The Hag and the wizard were in the kitchen. They had heard nothing but when they saw the children's faces they wasted no time.

'Only Ulf has the strength to shift the bridge,' said the Hag. 'He's upstairs with the ogre.'

They ran upstairs and burst into the ogre's bedroom. The ogre was dozing and Ulf was just covering him with a blanket.

'Ulf, come quickly – we're being attacked. We must pull up the drawbridge.'

Ulf wasted no time. He pulled the blanket further up on the bed, hoping that the ogre had not heard, and ran downstairs.

But the ogre had heard. The children were about to follow the troll downstairs when a great roar came from the bed. Then the blanket was thrown off, and after a few convulsions the ogre was on his feet.

'Oh, be careful!' said Mirella – for the ogre had not been out of bed for days.

The ogre swayed and clutched the bedpost. He straightened himself. He flexed his biceps – and the bulge of muscle rolled down his arm and grew bigger and bulgier by the minute. He lifted one leg, and put it down. Then he lifted the other – and kicked a chair which flew across the room . . .

'Attacking us, are they?' he roared. 'Attacking Oglefort! Get me my club and my entrenching tool. And my trousers,' he added as an afterthought.

'Boiling oil,' said the Hag, looking round hopefully. 'They used to pour boiling oil on invaders – but we don't have any. Only salad oil and not much of that. And you two must go down into the dungeons and hide,' she ordered the children. 'Mirella must keep out of sight.'

'Well I won't. I'm going to fight with everything I can find,' said Mirella. 'We can throw things off the battlements.'

It was ridiculous how little they had to defend themselves with – but it was hundreds of years since the castle had had been attacked. Ivo had found some fire irons; Mirella grabbed a footstool . . . The wizard had seized a marble bust of Germania's grandmother.

With all his might, Ulf pulled up the chain which held the drawbridge in place. To get into Oglefort now, the invaders would have to swim the moat.

The army had been advancing steadily, and now it took up its position in front of the castle. It wasn't quite the troop which had set out from Waterfield. It was, in fact, considerably smaller. Three members of the Royal Fusiliers had turned back when they saw the narrow bridge over the gorge which they had to cross. Two soldiers from the Household Guards had fled when a giant had come roaring out of a forest that they had to pass through – and the Soldiers of the Bedchamber were down to four very bedraggled-looking riders.

But the two princes who were married to Mirella's sisters were still mounted – and leading the charge. Prince Philippe on a black charger rode on the left flank. He had left his stamp collection at home and was waving his sword and shouting abuse. Prince Tomas, still sucking a peppermint, led the right flank. But Prince Umberto, who was meant to be at the head of the whole troop had somehow managed to get to the back. He rode a grey stallion who was tossing his head and fidgeting because the prince had no idea how to control him, and Umberto looked sick with fear.

'We come to kill the Ogre of Oglefort,' shouted Prince Philippe.

'And to free the Princess Mirella,' shouted Prince Tomas. 'Open the gates!'

Prince Umberto didn't shout anything because he was trembling too much, but Mirella, up on the roof, had caught sight of him.

'I'm going to be sick,' she said, as the horror of his courtship came back to her, and she vanished behind a chimney stack on the other side of the ramparts.

The soldiers looked up at the castle. It was frighteningly large but there did not seem to be any cannons pointing in their direction. Prince Tomas gave a command and the archers laid their arrows to their bows. But before they could shoot, there came a mighty roar from the battlements. Then an enormous figure, hideous and hairy, his huge arms raised threateningly, appeared and glared down at them.

The riders shifted in their saddles. Prince Philippe's horse took a pace backwards.

Silhouetted against the sky, the Ogre of Oglefort was a terrifying sight.

'How dare you try to invade my castle, you vile scum,' shouted the ogre. 'I spit on you! I'm going to tear you limb from limb. I'm going to devour you toe by toe and ear by ear and nose by nose.'

He picked up a floor mop and hurled it into the mass of troops and it dislodged a Fusilier who fell to the ground.

'I'm going to grind your guts like corn. I'm going to dig your tonsils into the ground.'

But if the soldiers were frightened, the children and the rescuers on the battlements were utterly amazed. An hour ago the ogre had been lying limply in his bed waiting for death – and now he was roaring and threatening. Surely he would have a heart attack and drop dead?

Prince Umberto, who was already right at the back, edged his horse further away. It was as though the ogre's power could somehow reach them even from the roof.

But Prince Philippe and Prince Tomas were made of sterner stuff. They repeated the signal to the archers and a volley of arrows sped towards the towering figure on the roof.

The arrows missed – and the ogre picked one up and scratched his armpits with it. Then he looked round for a weapon and Ivo handed him a coal bucket which he hurled with all his might into the army – and a member of the Household Guards cried out and fell to the ground. The troll had made a sling from a sheet. He put in a metal cooking pot and sent it flying towards the Soldiers of the Bedchamber. It glanced off a sergeant's arm and he cried out but managed to stay on his horse.

A second hail of arrows flew up to the roof – and missed again.

'Come on, you lily-livered, cow-handed imbeciles. How dare you attack Oglefort Castle which has stood for five hundred years. Just you wait till I get down there and crunch you up between my molars.'

But one of the Fusiliers had broken ranks and was setting his horse at the moat. He could not jump it, but he meant to swim it – and he shouted to his sergeant to bring reinforcements. If he could get into the castle by the back door, he had a good chance of rescuing the princess.

The horse, however, had different ideas. It stopped dead and the soldier shot over its head into the deep and slimy water.

Mirella, emerging from the shelter of the chimney stacks, looked down and remembered what Bessie had said about the weeds in the moat. Well, if the soldier drowned that was one less for the attack. But as the Fusilier's anguished face appeared above the surface and vanished again, she saw to her horror that it was somebody she knew. One of the servants who had been kind to her in the palace – the son of the carpenter who had helped her to make her ants' nest.

Without thinking, Mirella rushed down the curving stone staircase and out by the sally port. There was an old lifebelt fixed by a rope on a stand and she threw it with all her might into the water.

'Go back,' she shouted. 'The ogre will kill you if you come any closer.'

The soldier caught the lifebelt and held on but as he did so he saw Mirella. Here was his chance for fame and glory – he and he alone would rescue the princess. Instead of swimming back to the army he thrust out towards the castle side of the moat and grabbed Mirella's legs.

Taken by surprise, Mirella let go of the rope and stumbled – and he pulled her into the water.

'Hold on, Your Highness,' he spluttered. 'We'll soon have you safe.'

Ivo, who had gone round to the back to fetch some loose bricks for ammunition, saw what had happened.

'They've got her – they've got Mirella,' he shouted. 'I'm going down to help her.'

'No you're not,' said Ulf, grabbing him. 'They'll only get you too.'

But someone else was in the moat, swimming strongly towards the soldier and his burden. And when the Fusilier saw what it was he screamed in terror.

A great mouth had opened in front of him, a crimson cavern with fearsome yellowing teeth. A mouth belonging to the most dangerous mammal in Africa, who could snap people in half with one movement of its jaw.

'Watch out!' Mirella shouted to the soldier who held her in his grip. 'It's the Oglefort hippo – she's a killer!'

Mirella was right: it was indeed the hippopotamus. This gentle animal who wanted nothing except to live in peace had come lumbering up before the battle, and taken it on herself to patrol the moat.

There was no way the solider could have known that Bessie would have died rather than taste his horrid flesh. He saw only the gaping mouth, the terrible teeth, and he loosened his hold on Mirella and – still in the lifebelt – he struck out for the bank.

Mirella managed to swim back to the castle side of the moat but the bank was steep and slimy. As she struggled to get out, Prince Philippe rode over.

'Don't worry, my dear,' he called to her in a patronizing voice. We'll soon have you out of here and safe back home.'

'I don't want to be safe,' she spluttered. 'And I'm not going home.'

'She's been brainwashed,' said the Prince to his aide – and since no one could swim the waters of the moat while the wild hippopotamus patrolled it, he gave orders that a big tree nearby should be cut down to make a bridge.

'Then we'll be able to get her out of the water and storm the castle,' he said.

But Bessie was not the only animal who had come to help.

'We need more ammunition,' shouted the ogre – and vanished to return with a grandfather clock, an iron bedstead and an armchair which he sent crashing down from the battlements.

'Come any closer and I'll blister the skin off your backsides!' he roared.

'I've run out of boulders,' said the troll – and then he heard above his head Nandi's quiet voice and saw that the aye-aye, in spite of her terror of men, was on the roof above him prising off the razor sharp slates which she handed him, so that he could send them flying like knives through the ranks.

But the army stood its ground, and the arrows came steadily.

Ivo was standing between the Hag and the wizard. He had thrown a footstool, a bedpan and a set of fire irons and his aim had been good but what use was that? Mirella's white face, and her look of terror when she heard that her father's army was coming, wouldn't leave him.

'Isn't there any magic you can do?' he begged the Hag. 'Anything at all?'

The Hag turned, still holding the soup tureen she had been about to throw.

She saw Ivo's pleading face, and remembered the time she had told him about Gladys's treachery.

'I could be your familiar,' he had said. And later: 'Familiars serve for life.'

And what sort of an employer had she been, what sort of a witch?

The Hag, in the midst of the battle, examined her soul. Just because no one seemed to want magic any more, just because she was content to sit in the Dribble soaking her feet, she had let it go.

Ivo said no more. He only looked.

But could she in fact do any serious magic? Wasn't

her power all gone? Yet Ivo believed in her; she could feel his trust streaming towards her. On her other side, Dr Brainsweller was muttering something. It sounded like a spell. Was he trying to prompt her? Yes, he was . . .

The Hag threw the soup tureen, closed her eyes, called on the Great Witch of the Nether regions – and began to mutter.

And down below the soldiers started to bat away something with their arms, to make noises of disgust . . . One tore off his helmet to try and squash a thing which had appeared on his horse's neck. There were cries of, 'Ugh,' and, 'Disgusting,' and, 'Horrible, slimy things.'

There is nothing terrible in itself about frogs. One or two at a time can be pleasant to have about – but a whole host of them is different: frogs on the saddles, frogs in the arrow pouches, frogs on one's face – that is different. They got into the horses' ears, and were squashed under the horses' hoofs and slid down the necks of the riders – and as the soldiers looked upward they landed in their mouths.

'It's a very common spell,' said the Hag modestly, 'a Plague of Frogs, but it can be useful. This one came off well, I must admit.'

Mirella was still trying to climb out of the moat and two men, batting away the frogs, had begun to chop down the tree which was to make a bridge across the water. The marksmen, making noises of disgust as their hands encountered the slimy amphibians, went on firing.

Up on the ramparts, the wizard spoke a single word – and the Hag nodded.

'Yes,' she said. 'I can do those.'

Nothing happened at first – then the men who were chopping at the tree put down their axes.

'There's something on your nose,' said one.

'And there's something on your nose,' said the other.

They began to finger their faces, to make noises of disgust. The warts were enormous, with tufts of hair on them, and wobbly dark skin.

Shrieking with fear, they ran back to the rest of the army. Everybody was touching their noses now, looking at their reflections in the polished harnesses, pointing at each other.

All the soldiers were upset, but Prince Umberto, still at the back of the troop astride his charger, was almost out of his mind.

'What will my tailor say, and my hairdresser?' he squealed.

'There's witchcraft about,' said Prince Tomas.

Prince Philippe agreed but they had sworn to slay the ogre and bring back the princess, and once again both princes gave the signal to fire.

'Ow!' said Ulf – and put his hand to his shoulder.

It came away streaked with blood, but when the others rushed forward to help him he pushed them away.

'It's only a scratch,' he said. 'Trolls don't feel pain.' And he called up to Nandi for more tiles.

But the Hag was very upset. She and the troll had been friends for a long time. She took a deep breath, and turned to Ivo: 'The one I'm going to do now is a nasty one – very physiological. Are you all right with that?' And Ivo said, 'Oh yes! Please . . .'

The Hag muttered again – and, down below, the soldiers, ignoring the frogs and the warts, began to scratch themselves. They scratched their armpits and their heads and behind their knees – they tore off their doublets to get to their skin . . . They howled and twitched and cried out as their bodies turned into a fiery hell.

There are ordinary itches – itches you get from mosquito bites and sunburn. There are serious itches you get from eczema and chilblains and scabies. But The Great Itch, which the Hag had unloosed, was like none of these! After a few hours of The Great Itch, men are ready to leap into the sea and drown.

The ogre threw a kitchen table. Soon there would be no furniture left in the castle.

But now came the gnu. He trotted up slowly, because going to war was not to his taste, but he did not intend to fail his friends.

He came up behind the army – and as he drew closer he increased speed and put his head down . . . and choosing the largest horse with the strongest buttocks, he charged!

The horse was Prince Umberto's. It was a brave and fiery horse but being charged in the backside by a gnu was too much. The stallion reared, whinnied, swung round – and bolted from the battlefield.

The gnu pawed the ground and looked for another backside. He took care not to charge too hard for his quarrel was not with the horses but with the men who rode them. But the soldiers had had enough.

'We'll retreat to the top of the hill and then re-form for another attack,' ordered Prince Tomas, scratching like a flea-ridden monkey.

And gathering up their wounded as best they could, they rode away.

But they did not re-form. When they reached the crest of the hill the men, still itching madly, gazed upward and pointed to the sky. Flying above them towards the castle, was a swirl of dark shapes so terrifying that they could not even cry out.

In a moment they had urged their horses into a gallop and were out of sight.

And the ghosts smiled and glided on, making their way to the castle.

Twenty-Two
The Haunting

In the kitchen of the castle they were celebrating.

The ogre sat in his big carved chair, stuffing himself with anything the Hag could put on his plate.

'Shouldn't you start eating gradually?' she asked in a worried voice. 'You must have shrunk your stomach with all that refusing to eat, and you might be ill, suddenly filling it up.'

But the ogre said that was nonsense, the Ogres of Oglefort had cast-iron stomachs and he now felt absolutely fine.

'Repelling a whole army did me all the good in the world,' he said. And no one liked to suggest that it wasn't just he who had repelled the army but the Hag with her spells, and the animals, not to mention the troll and the wizard and the children manning the ramparts. They also wondered what would happen when the aunts arrived to attend his death bed and found him restored to health.

Meanwhile nothing could stop him from celebrating. The gnu and the aye-aye had been invited in, and the spider sisters hung down over the table by a specially long thread so that they could see what was going on.

'We showed them, didn't we?' said the ogre, gulping down the Hag's sloe cordial.

Only Mirella found it difficult to rejoice. Bessie had

147

helped her out of the moat by swimming underneath her and making a kind of shelf. She had changed out of her wet clothes and had had a hot drink – but seeing her father's army had frightened her badly and Umberto's stupid face, under the ridiculous helmet, wouldn't get out of her mind.

'What if they come back?' she whispered to Ivo.

'They won't. We really scared them,' said Ivo – and he looked proudly at the Hag who had shown herself to be a proper witch.

No one in the castle had seen what the army saw: a swirl of hideous black shapes flapping across the sky – and then dissolving into nothingness.

The ghost train had become a boat train for the first part of the journey. The Norns had sent it on the ferry to Osterhaven with the ghosts still inside – but once they arrived in Ostland they had been forced to glide to the castle under their own steam.

The long cold journey and the need to be invisible most of the time had annoyed them, but now they were settling in. They had found a suitable place for their headquarters – a clump of trees not far from the castle and close to a large mound of bones which seemed somehow familiar – and they were planning their special effects.

The Bag Lady had turned out her carriers and was rummaging with pale, plump fingers among the filthy clothes, looking for her corset. Being blinded by a corset often got people very upset.

The Honker was spitting steadily on to the grass. In spite of his age and the missing leg, his aim was still good.

The Aunt Pusher ran at an oak tree, his great hands held out in front of him, and the tree trembled and swayed.

'What's keeping him?' asked the Smoking Girl, lighting a fag from the stub of her old one. 'It's nearly dark.'

The Inspector had glided off on his own to investigate, which was his word for spying.

'You'd better unstick your jaws,' said the Man with the Umbrella to the Chewer. 'You can't grin properly with all that gum, and severed heads are no good unless they're grinning.'

The ghosts had been feeling quite cheerful, getting ready for the night's work, but now they felt a shivery kind of bleakness, and looking up they saw the Inspector.

His stony gaze travelled over them, taking in the Smoking Girl's untidy scarf, the Honker's crutch thrown on the ground.

'We leave in half an hour,' he said.

They all knew what to do; they had rehearsed it again and again. The rescuers must be punished, but the ogre must be killed – and killed absolutely. Only then would the ghosts get the reward they so yearned for – new stations, new junctions, new tunnels – perhaps even a new viaduct.

Their eye sockets glittering with greed, the ghosts took to the air.

It began with Charlie. He woke up in Ivo's bed with a yelp of fear and stood with his coat on end, shivering.

'What is it, Charlie?' asked Ivo sleepily.

149

Charlie leaped off the bed and disappeared under it, moaning pitifully.

Then there came a thud from next door.

Ivo went out into the corridor. It had been a warm night, but now there was an icy chill. Ulf always left a single lamp burning and the flame was flickering as though in a high wind. Then the door of the Hag's room opened, and she stumbled across the threshold, and fell to the ground.

'Don't,' she begged. 'Don't do that, I haven't hurt you.'

Running to help her, Ivo saw the dark shape of a man with enormous hands standing above her. He was so angry that he almost forgot to be frightened. What sort of a man pushed an old woman to the ground?

And then he realized. Not a man of course. Something different. And suddenly the corridor was filled with spectres. An old man glided past waving a crutch and Ivo felt a blob of something so disgusting on his face that he began to retch. This couldn't just be spit – this slimy, creeping, slithery nothingness which yet got into every crevice and hole.

These were not ordinary ghosts; they were something obscene and diabolical.

Mirella came out of her room, blinking, still half asleep, and saw Ivo bending over the Hag.

'What is it?' she asked. 'What's happening?' And then she cried out as she felt a steel spike digging into her shoulder.

'Steady on, she's the princess,' said the Aunt Pusher, floating in mid air. 'Must be. They didn't say there was a girl with the rescuers.'

150

'Can't be . . .' said the Man with the Umbrella. 'That's not how princesses look.' And he gave her another jab.

'Stop it! Stop it!' screamed Ivo, rushing towards her, but the Umbrella Man had seen Ulf coming out of his room and swooped towards him. Ghosts really hate trolls – their uprightness and strength – and he thrust the steel point of the umbrella into the troll's arms and chest and legs.

The wizard woke, sat up in bed, found himself staring at a grinning body-less head – and fainted.

Suddenly there was a kind of exodus – a swirl of phantoms along the passage towards the ogre's room. Punishing was one thing but now the killing had to begin.

It began quietly, with the ogre waking to find a girl sitting on his bed, draped in gauzy scarves. The ogre was surprised, but not displeased – and he sat up and said politely, 'Who are you?'

The next second he was fighting for breath, coughing uncontrollably – great racking coughs which shook his whole frame, while poisonous fumes poured into his lungs.

'Go away, you're horrible,' said the ogre.

He tried to bat away the Smoking Girl but his hand encountered only air. Not clean air, though. Sticky, malodorous, polluted air.

But an even more unpleasant woman now floated across the ceiling and from her upturned carrier bags there came a shower of filthy things: clothes or rags – the ogre could not be sure but they had a life of their own, a stink and a malevolent slinky way of floating down. And then one of them – something

151

unspeakable and elastic – wrapped itself round the ogre's face and blinded him.

The ogre had never seen a corset – Germania did not wear them – and he fought the ghastly garment bravely, but it was useless. It only wound itself more tightly around his eyes.

The children found him like this when they managed to reach him – staggering round the room tearing at something which covered his face. They ran to help him, snatching and pulling and tugging at the vile thing. It had no substance yet they could feel it, and smell it – it was the most horrible thing they had ever touched.

Able to see again, the ogre tried to make his way to the door, but before he had taken more than a few steps he slipped on a sea of spittle and heard the Honker's manic titter.

And now the real torture began. Every time he tried to get up the Aunt Pusher threw him to the floor and the Man with the Umbrella pierced him again and again, twisting the rapier point in his wounds.

'Ow! Ow! Ow!' yelled the ogre.

The troll had come in, ignoring his own injuries, and tried to help, but his healthy strength was no match for the spectres' evil nothingness and he found himself thrown back against the wall.

The phantoms were everywhere, filling the room with their hideous shapes – pushing, piercing, poisoning . . .

Then from a dark space above their heads, there came a disembodied voice.

'Cackle!' commanded the Inspector.

And the ghosts cackled! The cackle of ghosts is an

octave higher than the highest laughter of a human being and it is one of the most dreaded sounds in the world. Eardrums can be pierced by it, and the pain is unbelievable.

The children cried out in agony. The ogre put his hands to his ears and they came away stained with blood. Quite demented, he lurched out of his room and along the corridor to the stairs which led to the Great Hall.

Ghosts can kill a person by frightening him till his heart gives out – but they can also kill by causing a fatal accident. They followed the ogre gleefully. Leading from the Great Hall was a door that led to a long flight of steps to the courtyard. Steep stone steps, more than a hundred of them, down which a person could tumble and break his neck.

The ogre blundered round the Hall – shards of glass fell on him as the Honker batted his crutch into the chandelier. A lone brassiere fell from the Bag Lady's carrier and wrapped itself round the ogre's face so that he banged into the furniture – and still the ghosts kept up their dreadful cackling.

Everyone was in the Hall now – the Hag and the wizard had come stumbling in; anything was better than being alone. The children stood with their hands to their ears, paralysed with pain. When they were not torturing the ogre, the phantoms turned on the rest of them.

'No,' cried Ivo trying to warn the ogre, for he could see now that the ghosts had a plan – that they were pushing the ogre closer and closer to the flight of steps. 'Don't let them –'

But it was useless trying to warn the ogre, he could

hear nothing and the Aunt Pusher came up behind Ivo and sent him sprawling.

Suddenly the cackling stopped. It stopped completely, and the silence was so amazing that for a moment everybody forgot their wounds – and dared to hope that their torture might be coming to an end.

And it really seemed as if it might be so, for the ghosts were no longer attacking; they were standing quietly round the edge of the hall.

The ogre looked round, then tottered towards the couch with its bearskin cover and collapsed on to it.

The room darkened for a moment – and when they could see again the children saw that the ogre was not alone. There was a man sitting beside him. It was not easy to make out his shape but he seemed ordinary enough – he wore some kind of uniform and held a small gadget in his hand. If he was a ghost he did not seem to be a dangerous one.

But what was the matter with the ogre? The man had not touched him, yet the ogre's face was drained of every trace of colour and he fell back against the cushions and began to whimper like a small child.

The children clutched each other's hands. What was happening here?

The man in the uniform bent over the ogre and his lips formed just two words. Harmless words, surely, yet the ogre looked as though he wanted nothing except to die.

'Tickets please,' was what the Inspector had whispered.

But when the Inspector said, 'Tickets please,' he was not asking for tickets. He was pulling out the person's heart and soul, his dreams and his reasons for living.

Anyone the Inspector spoke to only wanted not to exist any more and Ivo closed his eyes because the look on the ogre's face was more than he could bear.

The Inspector vanished, the other ghosts surrounded their quarry – and now it was easy because the ogre had given up the fight.

They drove him to the top of the steps and he looked down. For a moment he hesitated – then a grinning dismembered head appeared suddenly in front of him and he lost his balance and went tumbling down and down and down, to land on his head on the hard stone below. The ghosts grinned in triumph and flew off into the night.

And yet the ogre was not dead. He should have been, but he wasn't. The troll, in spite of his open wounds, managed to help the ogre into bed and he lay with his eyes open and a look of utter bewilderment on his face. Nothing in his life had prepared him for this.

'They'll be back,' said the Hag. 'But another night will finish him. This isn't like his death bed, it's serious.'

She was pale and stooped and looked years older.

'It's the hatred,' said Ivo in bewilderment. 'Where does it come from? It's the hatred that's destroying him.'

Almost the worst thing was what had happened to Charlie. The little dog was still shivering, and twitching and juddering in a kind of fit. He refused food and even water and when Ivo tried to stroke him he bared his teeth.

155

'Be careful,' said Mirella. 'In the state he's in he might bite.'

'If Charlie bit me, I think I would die,' said Ivo.

The second night was even worse than the first. This time the cackling came at once, the maniacal ear-splitting noise as the phantoms swooped into the castle. Then came the stink of unwashed clothes, the poisonous fumes . . . and the violence as the ogre was pierced and pushed and thrown. More terrible even than the violence were the moments when the Inspector came close to them and they were pulled down into a dark pit of hopelessness, and wanted nothing except not to exist.

On the morning of the third day, everybody had given up hope.

The rescuers were huddled together in the ogre's room and they lay where they had fallen, like the victims of a battle. No one wanted to be alone – if the end was coming they wanted to be with their friends.

The ogre lay half in half out of his bed, one arm thrown over the covers. His breathing was shallow and irregular and he no longer spoke. The Hag had slumped down on the mat by the washstand; the troll and the wizard were stretched out beside the door.

It was all over. The ghosts would come once more, and this third visit would mean the end.

Mirella and Ivo were curled up beside each other. They were too tired to sleep, and were afraid to close their eyes.

After a while Mirella tried to sit up. 'Isn't there anything we can do?' she whispered. 'Not anything at all?'

Ivo shook his head. Mirella always thought there was something one could do, but sometimes there simply wasn't.

He began to doze off, then forced himself awake. 'Unless . . .' he shook his head. 'No. She wouldn't come for us. And anyway . . .'

But the children were so used to picking up each other's thoughts that Mirella understood him immediately.

'She might . . . if she knew how bad things were. But how could we let her know?'

'There'll be some words,' said Ivo. 'A spell.'

He tried to remember what he had seen in the encyclopedia in the days when he had read all about magic, but what came to his mind was Dr Brainsweller standing on the battlements and prompting the Hag. The wizard might not do much magic but he knew every spell there ever was.

But when they crawled towards him and managed to wake him up, the wizard shook his head.

'It's very secret,' he said. 'Very dark. Mustn't be used except in dire emergencies.'

The children only looked at him. He saw their pale exhausted faces, the bruise on Ivo's cheek . . . From the bed came the ogre's rasping breath.

The wizard struggled with his conscience. He would be giving away the secrets of his trade. And yet . . .

'Must . . . never reveal it . . .' he muttered. 'Never on pain of death.'

'We promise,' said both children. 'We swear on Charlie's head.'

The wizard leaned forward and whispered in their ears.

Darkness had fallen and the third night of haunting was about to begin. It would be the last night, the ghosts were sure of that.

'About time too,' said the Aunt Pusher as they stirred in their hiding place next to the burial mound. 'I never thought he would hang on as long as he has.'

It had been more work than they expected, this haunting, but now it was nearly over. And then home to their reward!

They began to rise into the air, but then something happened. There was a kind of stirring, an upheaval in the mound beside them: the bones fell away . . . and then out of an opening in the top there appeared a gigantic figure which stood glaring at the ghosts. Her hideous hairy face was set in an angry frown, her vast body shimmered in the evening light.

But what held the ghosts transfixed was her transparency. Mighty and enormous as she was, they could nevertheless see right through her. She too was a ghost – and suddenly they were very much afraid.

Germania cleared her throat and the ghosts trembled. An ogress clearing her throat is a sound like no other. It is a signal – a beginning of something that it is best not to know about.

'When I was a living ogress,' she said, raking them with her eyes, 'I could eat people. And now that I am a ghost ogress, I can eat ghosts. Now which one shall I start with?'

'No no, none of us,' gibbered the Man with the Umbrella. 'You wouldn't like us – No!' His voice rose in a shriek.

The ogress smiled. She took two paces forward. Then she put out her hand and fastened it round the Honker's ankle . . .

'I'll start with you, I think.' She picked up the crutch and threw it away. Then she opened her mouth, and with a howl of anguish, the Honker disappeared.

'Disgusting,' said the ogress, wiping her lips with her hand, 'but it can't be helped. Now who shall I try next?'

But now the ghosts were terrorized into action and one by one they rose into the air, trying to flee.

It did not help them. The ogress was ten times their size and had ten times their speed. She took off, still in the shroud she had been buried in, and went in pursuit.

As she rose, she snipped off the leg of the Man with the Umbrella, and sent the Bag Lady's carrier flying.

'I'll teach you to torment my husband,' roared the ogress.

'We won't do it again; we're going, we're going,' cried the Aunt Pusher. 'We didn't know.'

'If you come anywhere near this place again, I'll eat the lot of you.'

The ghosts took one last look at Germania and, shrieking in terror, they fled. But there was one phantom who was sure that he could escape the fate of the others. The Inspector, cocooned in his own darkness, began to slink away through the trees, keeping close to the ground.

The ogress stood still and sniffed. Then she took a

few giant steps forward, and her hand closed around him, and she brought him to her mouth.

Just for a moment after she swallowed him, Germania's stomach did not feel well; it gave a kind of blip of horror, a sort of spasm. She felt as though no food in the world was worth eating – never had been worth eating, and never would be worth eating again. That where her stomach with its happy memories had been there was now a pit of cold ghastliness – and the cold ghastliness would go on forever.

Then her ectoplasm got to work digesting the swallowed spectre, reducing him to a miasmic pulp – and Germania smiled because her stomach was itself again, and her work was done.

And she made her way back to the mound and climbed inside and the bones settled over her again – and all was peace.

Twenty-Three
Germania

It is a strange thing, but while the harm that ghosts do can be truly terrible, it does not last. As soon as the spectres have gone, the victims quickly recover. So within a few hours the children were able to run into the ogre's room and tell him that the ghosts had gone for good.

'And it was your wife that did it,' said Mirella.

'We were looking out of the window and we saw her,' said Ivo. 'There was a full moon and we saw everything. She chased them away and she ate some of them – she really is a marvellous woman.'

The ogre sat up in bed. 'I wonder how she knew,' he said. 'She's such a sound sleeper.'

The children looked at each other. They had promised the wizard they would keep his secret and the memory of that walk to the mound, with the ghosts so close, was one they did not want to remember.

'I must speak to her,' the ogre went on. 'She will be getting impatient. I must speak to Germania and tell her that I'm coming just as soon as the aunts arrive.' He threw out his arms like someone in a play. 'I must Give Myself To The Mound,' he said.

He went on saying that he must Give Himself To The Mound all the next day. He was still shaken and the marks made by the phantom umbrella had not quite healed, but as night fell, he put on his clothes.

161

Then he put his head round the kitchen door and in case they hadn't heard him before, he said once again that he was going to Give Himself To The Mound.

He was gone for over an hour. Though it was long past the children's bedtime, everyone was still waiting up in case he wanted to tell them how he had got on.

He came in silently and sat down. He drummed with his great fingers on the arm of his chair.

No one dared to say anything. The Hag handed him a mug of tea.

The ogre sighed. Then he sighed again. When he spoke his voice was full of bewilderment.

'She doesn't want me,' he said.

Everyone looked at him in a concerned sort of way.

'She *will* want me,' he went on. 'Later. But at the moment she feels like being alone. She says sharing a mound is like sharing a bed – you have to get used to it. That was why she appeared to me when I was about to change Mirella. I thought it was because she wanted me to come, but I was wrong – it was to tell me that she wasn't ready. And she thinks I should go away somewhere and enjoy myself.'

'Perhaps that's a good idea,' said the Hag. 'After all you're not old yet.'

'It isn't as though your wife doesn't want you,' said the troll. 'She just wants you *later*. A great many people feel like that.'

'Yes.' But the ogre was staring into space in a gloomy manner. 'Only I don't know where to go to enjoy myself. It's not really what I do.'

'I know,' said Mirella. 'You could go on a cruise. They're really good – you go to all sorts of places, and they play games on the deck.'

The ogre looked at her. Then his hand came down hard on the kitchen table. 'Of course! The fingernail boat. Just the thing. It's an old Viking ship made from the fingernails of dead warriors. The god Thor caused it to be built. It goes to all sorts of interesting places – the halls of the dead and the battlefields of heroes – and the passengers are people like me: ogres, satyrs, giants. You're right, I haven't been getting out enough.'

But though everyone thought that a cruise was a good idea they weren't so sure about a ship made of the fingernails of dead warriors.

'Don't you think you'd be better on a proper cruise liner – the *Empress of the Seas* or one of those,' said Mirella. 'Then you could throw rubber rings over nets and go to tea dances and things like that.'

The ogre said he would look into it. He was getting excited now, pacing up and down.

'The only thing is, what about the aunts?' said the wizard. 'They're coming because they think you're on your death bed and they're going to inherit the castle.'

'And so they are,' he said. 'So they are – one of them at least. I'm tired of owning things; I want to be free now. Completely free to circle the world until it's time to join Germania. I shall ask each of them to tell me what they would do with the castle if they inherited it and the one who comes up with the best plan shall have it. Now isn't that a good idea?'

They all agreed that it was. But of course for them time was running out. Whichever aunt inherited would want to be rid of them, that was for sure. Whipple Road was coming very close.

163

Though she dreaded the arrival of the aunts, the Hag now set herself to organize a great cleaning of the castle. Everyone helped, scrubbing and tidying and making beds. It was not an easy task because the ogre was now up and about and having 'good' ideas about how things should be done. He had not seen the aunts for many years and was excited at the thought of the reunion. Fortunately he spent a lot of time looking into different cruises and wondering what he should wear on board.

Though she was not fond of housework, Mirella made a point of helping the Hag: quite apart from anything else she wanted to make sure that no insects or spiders were swept into the dustpan. So it happened that three days after the battle, Ivo went on his own to finish off some digging in the herb garden – and found the gnu looking perplexed.

'Something's come up,' he said. 'Bessie's found something by the lake.'

So Ivo followed him to the far side of the lake and found the hippopotamus staring at something very unexpected.

'He's been here ever since the battle,' she said. 'He must have fallen off his horse and got left behind. I thought he'd wake up and go away but he hasn't. He's coming round now though, I think.' She bent over the figure lying on the grass and pushed him carefully with her snout. 'His horse is grazing over there. Funny-looking bloke, isn't he?'

Ivo agreed that he was. He had recognized Prince Umberto immediately. The prince's helmet had come off, his uniform was muddied, but there was no doubt that this was Mirella's suitor.

'You're right,' said Ivo to Bessie. 'He's coming round.'

Umberto was stirring. Now he opened his pale, vacant eyes and looked about him. He had dyed blond hair and a stupid face and Ivo understood at once that Mirella would rather do anything in the world than marry him.

'Eh . . . what the devil . . . where . . . ?' muttered the prince.

Ivo waited. Umberto must have had severe concussion, lying there for days. Perhaps he would have forgotten why he was here.

But he had not.

'Mirella,' he said, trying to sit up. 'Got to fetch her . . . Parents want her . . .' He rubbed his forehead. 'I want her too. Need her. Need her money . . .'

'Yes, of course you do,' said Ivo soothingly. 'Just wait here. I'll get you some water from the lake. It's quite clean – you're safe to drink it.'

He brought back a pitcher and watched as the prince drank, and spluttered, and drank again.

'Must find her,' he said, trying to get to his feet. And then, looking about him: 'I had a horse.'

'Your horse is safe,' said Ivo. 'You'll be able to ride back.'

But Umberto was getting very upset. 'Mirella . . . must find Mirella. Have to marry her. Have to because of no money.'

He started blundering about, muttering and peering, and Ivo watched him anxiously, wondering what to do. If Umberto found his way back to the castle, Mirella would go berserk; even seeing him

165

from the battlements had made her throw up. On the other hand, if he went back to the palace he might stir up the army again.

Ivo looked longingly at the lake. Pushing Umberto in would be easy enough and Bessie would see that he didn't surface again, but he hadn't really been brought up to murder people – even people as stupid as the prince.

It was as he was wondering what to do that he saw a white bird alight on the flat rock in the middle of the water. It was a large bird, very graceful and beautiful with a curved beak – a kind of gull, perhaps, or a tern, in from the sea. He wasn't sure what it was – but Mirella would have known.

And at that moment, Ivo knew exactly what to do.

He went up to the prince who had collapsed on a tree stump and bent over him.

'Listen, Your Highness, I've something to tell you. Something very special and important. Can you hear me?'

Umberto blinked and turned his head. 'Hear you . . .' he repeated.

'It's about Mirella. But you must be brave. You must prepare for a shock.'

'Shock . . .' muttered Umberto. It was not easy to tell whether he was still suffering from concussion or just thick.

'I know you love Mirella – you must do if you're engaged to marry her.'

'What? Yes, must do . . . Must love her . . .'

'And of course if you love somebody you want them to be happy, don't you?'

Umberto seemed to find this difficult to understand

166

but when Ivo had repeated it he nodded and said he supposed this was so.

'Well, Mirella is happy. She is happier than she has ever been in her life. Just look at her!' said Ivo throwing out his arm.

'Eh . . . What? . . . Where? . . .' The prince had stumbled to his feet.

'Over there. On that rock,' said Ivo. 'That bird. That's her. That's the Princess Mirella.'

The prince collapsed on to the stump again and rubbed his head.

'Don't understand,' he muttered.

Ivo put a hand on his shoulder.

'Do you know why Mirella came here to the ogre's castle? Because she came of her own free will, he didn't kidnap her.'

Umberto shook his head.

'Well, it was because there was something she wanted very much. She wanted it terribly. Have you any idea what it was?'

Umberto looked blank, which was not difficult for him, and said no he didn't.

Ivo lowered his voice in a reverent sort of way. 'She wanted him to turn her into a bird. She wanted to be a white bird flying high in the sky, free and alone forever.'

'Eh?'

Poor Umberto was completely out of his depth.

Ivo repeated his sentence. 'That is what she wanted more than anything in the world. To be a white bird. Only the ogre didn't want to change her, and he refused. But when he saw how brave she was on the battlements he decided to grant her wish. And yesterday, while you slept, he did it. Look,' he said, 'look carefully – can't you see how beautifully she flies – how free and happy she is?'

He pointed to the bird, which had most intelligently taken off from the rock, and was now making a graceful curve upward before winging its way towards the sea.

Umberto squinted at the sky. He couldn't see much because he was very short-sighted but he had got the message.

'White bird,' he repeated dopily. And then: 'Can't marry a bird. Wouldn't do.'

'No. You can't marry her. But you can go and tell her parents how happy Mirella is. How she has got exactly what she wanted. Maybe they'll give you a reward for bringing them such lovely news.'

Umberto smiled. One word had got through to him.

'Reward,' he said. 'Pay the tailor . . . pay the bookies . . . pay everyone . . .'

'That's right,' said Ivo. 'Now let's see if we can catch your horse.'

The horse had been at liberty for long enough. He wanted his stable, and he let himself be caught and mounted by the prince.

'Here, you can have my sandwich,' said Ivo, feeling in his pocket. 'Now you know where to go – over the hill and through that copse and then straight out the way you came. And remember how pleased they'll be when you tell them about Mirella.'

'Reward,' said Umberto, smiling his foolish smile, and Ivo watched as the prince rode away and out of sight.

Twenty-Four

The Aunts Arrive

'I suppose it might have been worse,' said Ivo. 'I mean they might have eaten people, like Germania used to. After all they are ogresses.'

But not much worse, because the aunts were thoroughly nasty. They had arrived the day before, stomping into the castle on their great feet – and had immediately started giving orders.

'You there,' said the Aunt-with-the-Ears, pointing to the Hag. 'I suppose you're the cook. I eat five times a day and my meals must be on the table the moment I appear.'

'I shall dig up my own meals,' said the Aunt-with-the-Nose, 'but I want my shoes cleaned with special polish – and the polish must NOT SMELL, do you understand?' she said, addressing the troll.

'You can carry my bag up to my room,' said the Aunt-with-the-Eyes, glaring at the wizard. 'But I will not be waited on by servants who have specks of dust on their clothes. Clean yourself up before I see you again.'

Then they handed the trolley over to Ivo and said, 'You and that girl there will look after Clarence. He must not get chilled.' The Aunt-with-the-Ears scowled at Charlie. 'And if that dog doesn't stop barking it'll be the worse for him.'

And as they stomped off to find the ogre, their

loud voices carried back to the rescuers.

'The first thing I'm going to do when I inherit the castle is get rid of those useless servants,' said the Aunt-with-the-Nose. 'I've never seen such a sorry-looking bunch.'

'What makes you think you're going to inherit the castle?' said the Aunt-with-the-Ears. She put her hands over the side of her face. 'Those spiders are making a quite unnecessary racket,' she muttered angrily. 'It's perfectly possible to spin a web without making a noise. The whole place is an inferno – I must find my earplugs. When I inherit I'm getting the place cleared.'

The Aunt-with-the-Eyes was peering disgustedly at the cracks in the flagstones. 'Full of dirt, full of dust. I can't live in a place like this. It must be scoured and scrubbed from top to toe before I move in.'

The ogre was waiting for them in his room and when they saw him all three aunts stopped dead.

'What are you doing out of bed?' asked the Aunt-with-the-Nose angrily. 'You said you were ill.'

'I hope we haven't come all this way for nothing,' said the Aunt-with-the-Ears.

'You do not seem to me to be dying,' said the Aunt-with-the-Eyes. 'I hope you haven't been playing a trick on us.'

The ogre was wearing a rather elegant dressing gown and underneath, though the aunts could not see this, was a pair of shorts which he had been trying on because he thought they would look good to wear on the deck of the cruise ship. He was a little bit hurt that the aunts were not pleased that he had recovered but he quickly reassured them.

'No, no. Not at all. I've decided to go away for a very long time. On a cruise. Germania thinks it would do me good. But altogether I don't want to own things any more. I want to lead a free and roaming life until it's time to get into the mound, so I'm definitely going to leave the castle to one of you. I thought you might like to have a week to look round the place and then come and tell me what you would do with it – and the person who comes up with the best idea shall have it.'

What was strange was that though the ogre's aunts were so unpleasant, Clarence was different.

'There's something really nice about him,' said Mirella, stroking his mottled shell.

'You feel that when he does hatch he'll have been worth waiting for,' said Ivo.

The animals too had the same feeling about Clarence. He was a good egg and much easier to look after than a baby with all those nappies and screaming and fuss – and Charlie seemed to agree for when the children moved away from Clarence he sat and guarded him.

But time was running out for the rescuers. If they had hoped that there might be one aunt who was less awful than the others, their hopes were unfulfilled. Whichever aunt inherited the castle it would be equally bad for them and they were determined to get away on the day the ogre left his home. They would have left earlier but the ogre had promised to send word to the boatman who had brought them that they needed to be fetched.

He himself had decided to leave in the hearse.

'Pity to waste it,' he said, 'and it'll make quite a stir when I get to the harbour.'

The hearse had turned out very well. Ulf had painted it black, and though the gnu had offered to pull it, Brod's cousin, the one who took messages, had a spare horse which he said they could borrow.

'Will you be all right in Whipple Road?' Ivo had asked Mirella. 'After all you used to be a princess and it's not very exciting.'

'Of course I'll be all right,' said Mirella.

But nobody felt all right during those last days. You can think you're prepared for something, but when it comes it can take you by the throat. The thought of leaving the castle, the gardens they had tended and the beautiful countryside was almost more than they could bear. Worst of all was the knowledge that they would never see their animal friends again – and the animals were taking it just as hard.

'I like being a gnu,' said the antelope. 'I'm *glad* to be a gnu – but I didn't expect that a gnu could feel such sorrow. It'll be a desert without you.'

The aye-aye was becoming very shivery and nervous again.

'It's as bad as when I was supposed to be Miss Universe with bananas on my head,' she said.

And she kept bringing presents down from the high trees for them: interesting feathers, bright berries and unusual twigs.

Bessie didn't say much but every so often she gave great spluttery sighs and shook her head.

And at night Ivo hugged Charlie and thought that if he had to go back to the Home he would die.

The adults felt it just as keenly. When she could

172

get away, the Hag sat on her stone in the Dribble and cried a little because it was hard to believe that she should find her Paradise so late in life, only to have it snatched away. The troll leaned his back against the five-hundred-year-old oak in his forest and tried to get used to the idea that soon he would again be trundling trolleys down the stuffy corridors of the hospital – and the wizard cooked in a frenzy, knowing that when he got back he would be trapped in his workshop trying to make useless things like gold, which nobody could eat.

Meanwhile inside the castle things were getting steadily worse. The three aunts sniffed and snooped along the corridors, they peered and poked into the rooms; they shuddered and shivered and complained. They found sordid tasks which they expected the rescuers to do.

'My ear plugs are too hard,' complained the Aunt-with-the-Ears, and she told the wizard to knead them with the soles of his feet to soften them.

The Aunt-with-the-Eyes had brought a bottle of ointment and a dropper which she expected the Hag to drop into her eyes and then yelled at her because it stung. The Aunt-with-the-Nose dug up patches in the lawn to get at the roots she liked for a snack and they had to follow her and put the turf back again.

One of the things they quarrelled about was where they would put their collections.

'There isn't a decent place for my worm collection anywhere,' complained the Aunt-with-the-Nose. 'I want somewhere warm and quiet and moist – that shouldn't be too difficult.'

The Aunt-with-the-Eyes wanted somewhere dry for her bone collection, and the Aunt-with-the-Ears said she needed a quiet, straw-lined place for her egg collection, and why didn't Dennis have anything like that. 'The place is big enough, surely,' she complained.

The children found it hard to keep their tempers, especially when the aunts bullied the Hag – but they were becoming very sorry for the ogre who looked more puzzled and worried every day.

'I'm sure they'll come up with something good soon, don't you think?' he asked them. 'They're just getting themselves sorted out.'

But as far as they could see the aunts were going to pieces. At the beginning they had been quite friendly to each other though rude to everyone else, but that had gone. They called each other names, they threw things and slammed doors, and at night they could be heard screaming in their sleep. Obviously each of them was so anxious to have the castle that their jealousy had become uncontrollable.

'I suppose I could leave the castle to all three of them,' said the ogre doubtfully, 'but with the way they're quarrelling now that doesn't seem like a good idea.'

Then there came a morning when the Aunt-with-the-Nose pushed the Hag out of the way so hard that she fell and hurt her forehead.

'Right,' said the troll. 'That does it. We're leaving straight away.'

The Hag said no, she was perfectly all right, but her friends had had enough. So they went to find the ogre and told him they were going – and they said

174

they were taking Charlie, which had already been agreed upon.

The ogre was very upset. 'Couldn't you wait just a few days? I could give you a lift in the hearse.'

It was difficult to say no to him but when they looked at the bruise on the Hag's forehead they knew it was time to go.

They went to bed early, meaning to start at dawn, but they had very little sleep because the aunts screamed and shouted all night and the Aunt-with-the-Nose was found sleepwalking in the corridor and had to be pushed back into bed. So they were later than they meant to be as they went to the ogre's room to say goodbye.

But when they got there they found a most extraordinary hullabaloo. All the aunts were standing round the ogre's bed and they were crying and screaming and hiccupping.

'I won't,' shouted the Aunt-with-the-Ears. 'I won't and you can't make me!'

'Well, you needn't think I will either,' yelled the Aunt-with-the-Eyes. 'I couldn't. I absolutely couldn't endure it.'

'And I suppose you think you can fob it off on me,' screeched the Aunt-with-the-Nose. 'But you can't. You can't. You can't,' she yelled, getting hysterical and stamping her feet.

'What's happened?' asked Ulf. 'What's going on?'

The ogre was sitting up in bed looking thoroughly bewildered.

'They don't want it,' he said, shaking his head. 'They don't want the castle. None of them do.'

The aunts turned on him.

175

'No we don't. We never will. We want to go home.'

'Home!' shouted the Aunt-with-the-Eyes. 'Home to my lovely lighthouse.'

'Home to my cave! My very own cave,' screeched the Aunt-with-the-Nose.

'Home to my abbey. Mine! My own place, my own home for ever and ever,' yelled the Aunt-with-the-Ears.

They had stopped screaming now and begun to sob – great gloopy tears of homesickness and relief.

It seemed that they had liked the *idea* of owning a castle but when it came to the point they couldn't bear to leave their homes and each of them had been foisting the castle off on the others, which was why they had been getting more and more bad tempered.

'Home to my roots and my stalactites and my worms,' cried the Aunt-with-the-Nose.

'Home to my cloister and my eggs and my quietness.'

'Home to the sea and my bones.'

They went on sobbing and slurping with relief for several more minutes. Then quite suddenly they said, 'Goodbye,' and rushed out of the castle. Rushed over the drawbridge and away . . . away over the hills, while the earth shuddered under their great boots.

But Ivo had remembered something. He ran out after them, ran like the wind – but there was no hope of catching up with them and after a while he came panting back into the ogre's room.

'They've left Clarence,' he said.

'They'll come back for him, surely,' said Mirella.

But they never did.

176

Twenty-Five
The White Bird

It was because of his horse that Prince Umberto returned safely to the palace in Waterfield.

The stallion simply plodded on, through dark woods, across dangerous bridges, on and on, not spooked by anything, making for his stable. All that Umberto had to do was hold on, which he managed just about, but when he reached Waterfield and the groom came forward to take the bridle, he slithered to the ground, almost fainting with exhaustion.

When he had pulled himself together and made his way into the palace, he found the whole family assembled in the big salon. The King and Queen were there, the Princess Sidony and her husband, Prince Philippe, were there, and so were the Princess Angeline and her husband Prince Tomas.

And they were all looking at a small blob in the centre of their circle.

The blob was not an ordinary blob; it was a very young baby. At one end the baby was having her nappy changed by Mirella's old nurse, at the other end the Princess Sidony was fussing with the baby's christening robe. Sweetie Pie had been born while her father was away fighting the ogre; she was a girl, and about to be christened in Waterfield Cathedral with a great deal of pomp and ceremony.

'Good heavens, it's Umberto,' said the Queen,

jumping to her feet. 'We thought you had been killed in the battle.' And then, 'Have you any news of our poor darling daughter? Have you any news of Mirella?'

'Yes I have,' said Umberto. 'I know exactly what has happened to Mirella. But you must prepare yourself.'

'Oh no!' The poor Queen looked stricken. 'The ogre has eaten her!'

'No. He hasn't done that. But he has . . . changed her. Mirella has become a bird. A white bird. I saw her, high in the sky.'

'Oh no! No!' cried the Queen. She burst into tears and so did Princess Sidony and Princess Angeline, while the King and the Princes looked utterly stricken.

But in the midst of the hullabaloo, the old nurse, who had finished with the baby's nappy, stood up and said, 'Now, now, there's no call for all that fuss. Mirella wanted to be a bird from when she was very small. She was always on the roof staring up at them. She'll be as happy as can be, so let's have no more weeping because she's got exactly what she wants and let's get this baby off to the church.'

It took time for the Queen to stop weeping, but Angeline then said, 'It's true, Mother. What Nurse says is true. Mirella never fitted in, you know that. Look at the fuss she made when she had to be a bridesmaid at my wedding.'

Prince Philippe and Prince Tomas nodded. To tell the truth they were terribly relieved that there was no question of another expedition to rescue Mirella from the ogre.

But Umberto had had a good idea. Obviously he

178

couldn't marry Mirella now, but he still desperately needed the money that Mirella's father had promised him if he married into the family.

He looked down at the crib where Sweetie Pie was lying, blowing bubbles and looking really rather nice.

'I suppose I could get engaged to her,' he said, pointing to the baby. 'I don't mind waiting.'

But Umberto was unlucky. Sidony let out a shriek of anger, Prince Philippe snorted and the King said, 'Most certainly not.'

Sweetie Pie wasn't going to be a difficult and strange girl like Mirella – they would find a far more suitable husband for her when the time came.

So Umberto went back to his homeland where his tailor and his barber and his bookie and all the people he owed money to were waiting for him, and his father said, 'Enough is enough,' and banished him to two dark rooms at the back of the palace where Umberto had to do all his own housework – he even had to wash his own bedsocks.

But the people of Waterfield, and the school children in particular, could never hear enough about Mirella. They became keen bird watchers and bird protectors – bird tables and bird feeders appeared everywhere in the town and the King and Queen had a special flag made, which flew over the palace, that showed a white bird with outstretched wings.

And again and again the children would nag for stories of Mirella.

'Tell us about the Princess Mirella,' they would beg their parents. 'Please tell us about the Princess Who Flew Away.'

Twenty-Six
Return of the Ghosts

The ghosts were back in their train, going round and round in an everlasting circle. They had been promised that if they frightened the ogre to death, their train would be re-routed – they would go on branch lines, through junctions, into different tunnels – but they had failed, and now they were doomed once again to travel on the same wearying line.

The Ghost with the Umbrella had lost a leg. Ghosts don't feel pain, but it was inconvenient and he had to use his umbrella as a crutch. The Honker's seat was empty and the dark place where the Inspector used to hover was gone.

Their failure weighed heavily upon the remaining ghosts. They were doomed to go round and round forever. There was nothing to be done.

But in their cave, the Norns now woke.

They didn't wake very much; they were too far gone, but they woke as much as they could and gradually they remembered what had happened.

They had sent the ghosts to frighten the ogre to death.

'Screen!' screeched the First Norn.

And: 'Screen! Screen!' croaked the Second and Third Norns.

So the magic screen was brought and the Norns

peered into it. They were so exhausted they could only just make out the pictures.

First the castle . . . then the castle courtyard and a strange sort of carriage waiting to cross the drawbridge. The carriage was closed and painted black with a white skull on the side, and the words: 'Here lies Dennis of Oglefort. Rest in Peace.'

'A hearse!' cried the First Norn.

'A funeral hearse,' said the Second Norn.

'Going to the graveyard,' said the Third.

They blinked excitedly at each other.

'Ogre dead!' said the First Norn.

'Ogre finished,' said the Second Norn.

'Being buried,' said the Third Norn.

They went on peering at the screen as the hearse lumbered away across the drawbridge, carrying the remains of the wicked monster to his grave.

'Princess free?' wondered the First Norn.

'Saved?' said the Second Norn.

'Back home?' wondered the Third.

They peered at the screen again and the picture changed . . . flickered . . . and then stopped in a walled garden with beautiful flowers and grass. The Princess Mirella was bending very carefully over a deep red rose, smelling the blossom just as a princess should. Her hair was combed and she looked very happy.

The Norns smiled. They didn't often smile and the effort cracked the sides of their mouths but it didn't matter. The princess was safe, all was well and they could sleep – not just for weeks or for months, but for years and years and years.

Their eyes were closing when they remembered the ghosts. They had not given them their reward for killing the ogre. With a great effort they got back on their knees and waved their withered arms.

And in the train, the spectres sat up and gasped with amazement. The train had reached one of their usual stations on the dreary circle line, but it did not go on to the next station, and the next, round and round and round.

No, it took off on a completely different route. It went whizzing off on a branch line that they had never seen, and then a junction, before it changed direction once again. New stations, new junctions, new tunnels – even a viaduct – unfolded before the spectres' amazed eyes, as they were rewarded for something they had definitely not done.

'Perhaps we should become better ghosts?' suggested the Man with the Umbrella. 'Less beastly and so on.'

But no one thought this was a good idea.

'We're used to being horrible and vile,' said the Aunt Pusher. 'Anything else would unsettle us.' And they went on staring at this new world that had unfolded before their evil eyes.

But the Norns by now were fast asleep, and as they slept the floor of the cave sank slowly down and down, ever deeper into the Underworld, and the nurses and the harpies sank down with them, because their work was done. And in Aldington Crescent underground station all was silence and all was peace.

Twenty-Seven

Gladys Again

'Good heavens,' said Mirella, looking out of the kitchen window. 'Who on earth is that?'

A man in a grey business suit was coming slowly over the drawbridge, looking about him nervously.

Ivo stared. 'I think it's Mr Prendergast,' he said, 'the Hag's lodger in London,' and ran out to meet him.

Ivo was right. Without a single magic bone in his body, and without the help of the Norns, Mr Prendergast had managed to make his way to Oglefort because he had something he wanted to give the Hag. It was a wooden box, and when the Hag opened it, she found a very small urn filled with ashes.

'It's Gladys,' said Mr Prendergast simply. 'She passed away peacefully in her sleep so I had her cremated and I thought she would like to come to you.'

Everyone was very touched and the children suggested there should be a proper ceremony and a scattering of the ashes, perhaps near Germania's mound, for company. But the Hag shook her head.

'We began together in a Dribble, Gladys and I,' she said, looking down at the little urn in her hand. 'And she shall end in one.'

So that afternoon she went alone with her toad to her favourite place in the world, and sat on the stone in the middle of the marsh, and though she was sad, her sadness was mixed with relief – because she could now forgive Gladys completely for having said she was too tired to come to the meeting. Gladys must have been much nearer the end of her life than the Hag had realized, and had every right to be tired. And really nothing but good had come out of it all because they had found Ivo, and there couldn't be anything better in the world than that.

Mr Prendergast had brought news too about the wizard's mother. Mrs Brainsweller had got a very important job, organizing all the Banshee choirs which went to wail at places where something bad had happened. This meant travelling all over the country and she had decided to leave her son to get on with his own life.

'I did my best for him,' she had told Mr Prendergast. 'But he was never properly grateful – and really when I saw him making a *salad* I realized I was just wasting my time.'

This news was a tremendous relief to the wizard, and to the two spiders who had been watching over him, and that night he cooked a wonderful festive meal for everyone using produce from the garden and they drank to Gladys's memory and toasted 'Absent Friends'.

When it was clear that the aunts were gone for good, the ogre had asked the troll to take care of the castle till he returned, but this time Ulf had been firm.

'We'll stay but only if you leave the castle to us when you go and join Germania in her mound. We have the children's future to think of.'

184

The ogre had agreed and sent for a lawyer to make a proper will. He had also left them his sock drawer so there was money to run things properly and gradually more people came to the castle, not to be changed into animals but to work and to help. Brod sold them a cow and some chickens, and his little grandson came whenever he could to lend a hand. Mr Prendergast was so sad at the thought of making the dangerous journey back and living alone in Whipple Road that he decided to stay. He did the accounts and was useful in all sorts of ways and the Hag wrote a letter to the Principal of the Children's Home saying that Ivo was safe and well, and the orphanage could have her house and sell it and keep the money. She was sure that this would keep the Principal quiet – and she was quite right.

They had postcards from the ogre quite often; he was really enjoying life on board the *Empress of the Seas*. He had turned out to be the best at deck quoits and won a prize at bingo, and the Captain had invited him to sit at his table.

'I don't think the fingernail boat would have suited me nearly so well,' he wrote.

There was some talk about starting a school, but the children thought this was a bad idea.

'Anyone who can read and write and add and subtract can educate themselves,' said Ivo firmly – and somehow the talk died down.

The Norns were mistaken when they looked into the screen and thought that Mirella was smelling a rose. She had in fact been settling the spittle bug she'd taken from the ogre's ear into the centre of the flower, which was damp and quiet and suitable.

'I don't think the other passengers would like it if you had insects coming out of your ear all the time,' she had told the ogre. 'And you know I'll look after them.'

Which she did, most faithfully. Everyone was careful not to make the garden too tidy and to leave heaps of compost and a few stones, and some leaf mould so that there was always somewhere for the woodlice and bugs to go, and it became a sanctuary for everything that crawled and buzzed and flew.

'Oh, we are lucky to be able to grow up here,' said Mirella.

'To live here forever if we want to,' said Ivo.

They were in the garden on a lovely autumn afternoon. The gnu grazed peacefully nearby; the aye-aye was sitting on the roof of the greenhouse peeling a cob of sweetcorn they had brought her; they could hear Bessie splashing in the lake.

And on a sunlit patch of grass sat Clarence on his trolley. The aunts had not come back for him and he was part of the family now. Charlie, as always, was guarding him and from time to time he carefully licked the mottled shell. Clarence was obviously going to take his time to hatch, and whether he was going to be someone who would save the world or just an outsize chicken, nobody knew, but the children were not in a hurry.

Anyone who has an egg to watch over has a stake in the future, and the future – they were sure of it – was going to be *good*.

THE END

Turn the page for an extract from

MOUNTWOOD SCHOOL FOR GHOSTS

by exciting new storytelling talent

TOBY IBBOTSON

Based on an original idea by his mother, the late, great

EVA IBBOTSON

Percy

The next day when Daniel came home from school, his new neighbours had arrived. They were called Mr and Mrs Bosse-Lynch, and Daniel's Great-Aunt Joyce, who had been spying from her window all day, was very satisfied. They had the right sort of car, and the right sort of clothes, and Mr Bosse-Lynch had started trimming the hedge immediately. Then two ladies from the town had arrived to clean the house, and Great-Aunt Joyce had heard Mrs Bosse-Lynch telling them what to do before they had even got through the door.

That night, when Daniel had put his light out and lay in the darkness waiting for sleep, he heard something. At first he thought that it must be a pigeon under the slates. But it wasn't the right cooing and scratching noise that pigeons made. It seemed to be coming from the wall beside his bed. On the other side of the wall, he knew, was an attic room just like his in the house next door. The noise was more a snuffling or gulping kind of noise. He sat up and put his ear to the wall. Now he could hear quite clearly. He heard

3

stifled sobs, and sniffs. Someone was crying.

Daniel lay down again and tried to think. Perhaps Mrs Bosse-Lynch was secretly a very tragic person, with a horrible sad secret that she crept up to the attic and cried about at night. He hoped not, because he didn't want to feel sorry for someone whom horrid Great-Aunt Joyce approved of. But it was far more likely that they had a prisoner in the attic. They had kidnapped someone, probably a rich man's daughter, and sneaked her into the house. Soon they would cut off her ear and send it to the desperate parents. On the other hand, it could be a poor mad relation whom they didn't want anybody to know about. Daniel's friend Charlotte had read a book about someone like that. It was called *Jane Eyre* and was one of her absolute favourites.

Either way, Daniel had to make contact. He sat up again and knocked three times on the wall. The sniffling stopped.

'Hello, who's there?' he called. 'Do you need help?'

Still there was no sound. But then part of the wall slowly went soft and bulgy. The bulge got bigger, and separated itself from the wall. It was swirly and colourless, almost transparent. Then parts of it started taking shape, a hand appeared here, a leg there. The air in the room was suddenly icy cold, and in front of Daniel stood a small boy in a nightshirt,

4

with golden curls and big weepy eyes.

'You are a ghost, aren't you?' said Daniel. 'I thought you were someone in trouble.'

'I am someone in trouble,' said the ghost, and huge ghostly tears started to roll down its cheeks. 'I am someone in terrible trouble.'

'I think I saw when you came,' said Daniel. 'You were in the removal van.'

'Yes, I was,' said the ghost. 'It wasn't a bus.' The tears rolled ever faster down its pale cheeks.

'Of course it wasn't a bus, it was a removal van.'

'But I thought it was,' gulped the ghost. 'And I don't know where I am and I don't know where Father and Mother are and—'

'Please try to stop crying,' said Daniel. 'And keep your voice down or you'll wake Great-Aunt Joyce.'

The ghost was obviously a young child, and seemed to be working himself into hysterics. 'If you calm down and tell me about it, I might be able to help.'

Daniel was secretly a bit disappointed. Ever since the arrival of the removal van he had been hoping for something really shockingly ghastly, perhaps a leering headless skeleton or a viciously grinning ghost murderer who dissolved his victims in acid. Anything really that would scare Great-Aunt Joyce to death, or at least make her flee from Markham Street

5

and never return. But if she came up now and saw this weeping boy, she would probably just slap him and shoo him out.

However, even a small sad ghost is better than no ghost at all, and Daniel was a kind person and more than willing to sort out his problems if he could.

'You'd better tell me the whole story,' he said, and Perceval, for that was his name, came and sat on the bed and began.

Percy told his story with lots of pauses for miserable sniffing and cries of 'Oh, what am I to do?' and 'I shall be alone forever!', so it took him quite a long time.

Percy and his parents, Ronald and Iphigenia, had materialized in good time at the service station, where they had met up with Cousin Vera and the other ghosts and spectres who had applied for Mountwood School for Ghosts. There was quite a crowd milling about the parking bay where the bus was to pick them up. Some of them were old acquaintances, and they hung about, chatting, catching up on each other's news. After a while, when the bus still hadn't come, Percy had got bored and wandered off. There were lots of great big lorries standing silent and dark in the parking area. Percy glided among them, peeping in sometimes to look at the drivers snoring in their cabs. They had little beds with curtains, which reminded Percy of when he had been alive and his mother had read poetry to him before he went to sleep. His favourite one had started, 'Where the bee sucks there suck I.'

When Percy got back to the pick-up place, he saw a bus standing in the parking bay, revving its engine. There were no ghosts to be seen. He cried, 'Help, help, wait for me! Don't leave without me!' and threw himself through the side of the bus just as it drew away and rumbled off into the night.

'But it wasn't a bus,' said Percy sadly, looking with at Daniel with tragic eyes. 'The bus had already left.'

'Well, why didn't your parents wait for you? They must have been worried sick when you didn't show up.'

'I don't know, I don't know. I have been aba . . . adn . . .'

'Abandoned.'

'Y-y-yes. Like the Babes in the Wood.' Percy collapsed in hopeless weeping.

When he had recovered slightly Daniel said, 'I still don't see how you could mistake a removal van for a bus.'

'But I've never *been* on a bus. And it had words on the side like where we were going.'

'What do you mean?'

But Percy could speak no more. With a final wail

of 'Poor me! Oh, sad unhappy me!' he threw himself face down on the bed.

Daniel heard Great-Aunt Joyce's bedroom door opening, and her tread on the stair.

'That's done it,' he said.

'I'll disappear,' said Percy. 'I'm quite good at it.' And he started to fade, vanishing just as Great-Aunt Joyce appeared in the doorway.

Daniel turned on his bedside light. Great-Aunt Joyce was wearing a flannel dressing gown and tartan slippers, and her hair was in curlers. She looked very angry, and peered around the room.

'Really, Daniel, this is appalling. What on earth is going on? I must have silence after my pill. I shall be speaking to your father.'

'Oh, it's you, Great-Aunt Joyce. I was having a terrible nightmare.'

'Were you now?' said Great-Aunt Joyce suspiciously, and it seemed to Daniel that she stared intently at the exact spot where Percy had just vanished. 'A nightmare, was it? That's what comes of not chewing your food properly. Poor digestion.'

When she had gone, a small voice spoke from the empty bed.

'She doesn't seem very nice,' said Percy.

'She isn't. We'll have to be absolutely quiet now, Percy. We'll talk about this tomorrow.'

THE BEASTS OF CLAWSTONE CASTLE

EVA IBBOTSON

*'They ought to be in the country,' said Mrs Hamilton.
'It's where children ought to be.'*

When Madlyn Hamilton and her younger brother
Rollo are sent by their mother to stay with their
Uncle George at crumbling Clawstone Castle, they
can see that action is needed before the castle falls
down completely! With the help of a team of
scary ghosts – including Mr Smith, a one-eyed
skeleton, and Brenda the Bloodstained Bride – they
hatch a spooky plan to save their new home. But
with a sinister scientist after the estate's prize
cattle, money might not be enough to save the
mysterious white beasts of Clawstone Castle . . .

THE SECRET OF PLATFORM 13

EVA IBBOTSON

'Well, this is it!' said Ernie Hobbs, floating past the boarded-up Left Luggage Office and coming to rest on an old mailbag. 'This is the day!'

Platform 13 at King's Cross Station hides a remarkable secret. Every nine years a doorway opens to an amazing, fantastical island and its occupants come visiting. But the last time the doorway was open the island's baby prince was stolen from the streets of London. Now, nine years later, a rescue party, led by a wizard and an ogre, is back to find him and bring him home. But the gentle prince seems to have become a spoilt rich boy, and he doesn't believe in magic and *doesn't* want to go home. Can they rescue him before the doorway disappears forever?

WHICH WITCH?

EVA IBBOTSON

*'And remember,' he said, throwing out his arms,
'that what I am looking for is power,
wickedness and evil. Darkness is All!'*

Arriman the Awful, feared Wizard of the North, is
searching for a monstrous witch with the darkest
powers and is holding a sorcery competition to
discover which witch is the most fiendish.
Glamorous Madame Olympia conjures up a
thousand plague-bearing rats, while Belladonna,
the white witch, desperately wants to be a
wicked enchantress, but only manages to
produce flowers not snakes. Can she become
more devilish than all the other witches?